The North Hollywood Detective Club

in

The Case of the

Christmas Counterfeiters

Mike Mains

Preface

"I offered you an opportunity to partake in my little enterprise, but you wouldn't listen. Very well. Now you'll have to die."

With those words, the one-eyed man stepped out of the vault and the heavy steel door swung shut.

"Wait," cried Jeffrey Jones, but it was too late. He heard the combination lock turn. He and his friends were locked in the airtight vault.

Pablo Reyes rushed to the inside of the vault door and grabbed hold of the cold metal handle. The cordlike muscles on his forearms strained as he pushed, pulled, twisted and turned, but it was no use. The door wouldn't budge.

He stopped and stepped back, his face flushed and his chest heaving. "We're trapped," he said. "Trapped like rats."

"At least until somebody finds us," said Marisol Rodriguez. She brushed black hair back over her ear and looked from one boy to the other. "I mean, eventually someone will have to find us, won't they?"

Jeffrey slumped against the side of the vault and slid down to a seated position on the concrete floor. "It's worse than that," he said.

Marisol watched him carefully. "What's worse?"

Jeffrey felt a sick churning in his stomach. He looked into the hopeful eyes of his young friends, but he didn't have the heart to tell them.

Pablo kneeled down next to him. "What is it, Jeffrey?"

"He said we have to die. That means he set the timer."

"What timer?"

Jeffrey straightened his glasses and looked up at his friends. "This vault comes with a safety mechanism. It's designed to go off in case of a break-in, but it's also connected to a timer which can be set in the next room. When the safety mechanism is activated, the vault is flooded with poison gas."

Marisol gasped and covered her mouth. Pablo's face glazed white as a sheet. An intercom buzzed and they heard the voice of the one-eyed man coming from a loudspeaker. "Can you hear me, boy? If you can, press the intercom button on the wall."

Jeffrey leapt to his feet and pressed a red button on the wall by the vault door. "I can hear you." Pablo and Marisol crowded in close behind him, shoulders touching. They waited for the man's response.

"I've set the timer for midnight, exactly fifteen minutes from now. That's all the time I need to make my escape. If not, I can use your young lives as leverage. Of course, at this point, I fully intend to get away. I wish I could tell you that the gas is painless, but it's not. It's excruciatingly painful." The man chuckled. "I could describe to you the unspeakable agony you will soon experience, but perhaps it's better if you imagine it for yourselves. No one will save you and no one will hear you scream. Goodbye."

The intercom buzzed and went dead.

Marisol screamed.

Pablo leaned over Jeffrey's shoulder and jammed the red intercom button. "Hey! Hey! Come back!"

Jeffrey took off his glasses and covered his face with his hands. There was no way out. He was going to die and his friends were going to die, and everything was his fault. He felt himself panicking and his mind went blank. How did it happen? How did they get there? Then he remembered …

Chapter One - 17 Days Before Christmas

Jeffrey and Pablo were clearing leaves from Mrs. Martin's backyard when they found the body. Jeffrey stumbled back, lost his footing, and fell on his backside into a pile of red and brown December leaves. Pablo stood completely still and stared at the body. "Is he dead?" he asked.

Jeffrey rose from the crumbling leaves and shook his head. A harsh morning wind blew sharply across his face. A scratchy rendition of *O Tannenbaum (O Christmas Tree)* spilled out from Mrs. Martin's decrepit old house at the far end of the yard. The elderly German woman lived there alone, hidden behind the peeling paint, the creaky front porch, and the old wooden shutters that banged against the house when the wind howled. The entire property was covered by trees and vines and overgrown bushes, everything dark and hidden and in the shadows. To Jeffrey, it was the perfect location for a murder.

He approached the body cautiously, leaves crunching under his shoes.

"He looks dead," Pablo said.

The man's body was face down and half hidden under a layer of leaves. The boys kneeled at his side and shook him gently.

When they received no response, they rolled him over, making a crackle among the leaves and dead twigs.

The body belonged to a young Asian male in his early twenties. Leaves and small twigs clung to the sticky blood that matted his shirt. Underneath, two enormous bullet holes perforated the young man's chest, leaving only a bloody pulp.

Jeffrey felt a rumbling in his stomach and a rush of putrid hot liquid flooding up to his throat. He turned his head to the side and choked on the vomit that stuck in his throat.

Pablo winced at the sight of the man and the smell of blood that twitched at his nostrils. He glanced at Jeffrey. "You okay, man?"

Jeffrey coughed and nodded. When he turned back to the bloodied body, his own face was pale and glistening with sweat. He straightened his glasses and studied the young man's face.

"He looks Chinese."

"You can tell?"

Jeffrey nodded. "He's a gang member, too."

Pablo's eyebrows went up.

Jeffrey pointed to a triangle of three dots tattooed on the man's face, below the corner of his left eye. "The first dot stands for life, like a lifetime commitment. The second dot stands for prison. The third dot stands for death. By joining the gang, he's agreeing to a lifetime of prison and death."

Pablo grimaced. "Man, that's messed up."

"That's how some people choose to live."

"Not me."

Jeffrey reached for the man's wrist. His hand trembled as he felt for a pulse and his eyes widened behind his glasses.

"He's alive!"

In a second the two boys were sprinting across the four-acre yard to the old house where Mrs. Martin lived. A Christmas tree, decorated with candy canes and antique ornaments, stood proudly in the window. The Christmas music blaring from the house grew louder as they neared.

Pablo reached the porch first and leapt up the wooden steps. He banged on the frame of the screen door. Then he jammed the doorbell, again and again. The music coming from inside the house was deafening.

An old woman's muffled voice shouted over the music and the bell. "Who is it?"

"It's me! Pablo!"

Jeffrey caught up and stopped at the foot of the porch steps. He was a stocky boy, unaccustomed to running, and he heaved for air.

"She's coming," Pablo told him.

Jeffrey nodded. He bent at the waist, took off his glasses and wiped his face with his sleeve. Using the handrail, he lumbered up the wooden steps.

A phonograph needle screeched across vinyl and the music stopped. Floorboards creaked inside the house, followed by the unfastening of a door chain, the turn of a deadbolt, and the un-locking of the door. It swung open and old Loretta Martin, dressed in a ratty yellow bathrobe, faced them from behind the screen door. Behind her, the inside of the house was dark. Both boys talked at once.

Mrs. Martin put up her hands and spoke with a thick German accent. "Wait, wait! I can't hear when you talk at the same time!"

"We found a body," Pablo began, breathlessly.

"He's alive," Jeffrey added, and pointed across the yard. "Call the police and tell them to send an ambulance."

"You found a body? In *my* yard?"

"Yeah, he's covered with blood," Pablo said.

The woman's eyes opened wide.

"Call 9-1-1," Jeffrey told her. "Hurry."

Mrs. Martin stood staring at them.

"Did you hear me?" Jeffrey said. "Call 9-1-1."

The woman blinked.

"Why are you standing there?" Jeffrey shouted. "Call the police."

The old woman gasped and disappeared in the house. Jeffrey craned his neck, trying to peer past the screen door to see where she went.

"You're scaring her," Pablo whispered.

"She should be scared. There's a body in her backyard." He saw Pablo's disapproving look and added, "If one of us had a phone, we wouldn't have to do this."

Pablo nodded. Neither his parents nor Jeffrey's would allow them to have a phone until they turned sixteen.

Jeffrey shouted into the house, "Are you calling the police?"

A scraggly voice called back. "I'm calling my grandson."

"What? No!" Jeffrey banged on the door frame.

Pablo grabbed Jeffrey's arm and steadied him. He called inside the house. "Mrs. Martin, why don't you let me in? I'll call the police."

The woman appeared back behind the screen door, looking frail and frightened.

"Who are you?"

"It's me, Pablo. We're cleaning your yard, remember? Look, there's a man in your backyard who's hurt. Would you let me in so I can call the police?"

Mrs. Martin reached for the latch on the screen door. Her withered hand shook with age as it grasped the latch and turned it.

Pablo pulled the screen door open and stepped into the house. "Thank you."

"Not *you*," Mrs. Martin said to Jeffrey, and she led Pablo into the house.

Jeffrey stared back at the screen door, his nostrils flaring. He was mad at Mrs. Martin for being old and senile. He was mad at his parents for not letting him have a phone. He was mad at life for always being so unfair. Just about every kid at his school, except for him and Pablo and a few others, had their own phone. If he had a phone right now he could call the police himself and possibly save a man's life. He turned away from the door and stomped on the wooden porch.

The screen door creaked open behind him. He turned to see Pablo stepping out of the house.

"I called the cops," Pablo said. "They want us to stay. Let's get back to the body." He started down the porch steps.

"Hold on a second."

Pablo stopped.

"Let's try to figure out when that guy was shot," Jeffrey said.

Pablo checked his watch. "We got here at seven-thirty and it's eight o'clock now. That means he's been laying in that yard for at least half an hour. He must have been shot early this morning, before we got here."

"My guess is he wasn't shot here at all," Jeffrey said. "He was probably shot somewhere else and then dumped here. Otherwise Mrs. Martin would have heard the shots."

"Not with that music playing. She had it blasting. Plus that body's clear at the end of the yard."

Jeffrey nodded. "Good points."

Mrs. Martin appeared back behind the screen door, watching them warily.

Jeffrey turned to her. "Mrs. Martin, did you hear any gunshots this morning?"

The old woman shook her head.

"How about last night?"

"No."

"What time did you start playing music this morning?"

"Why are you asking these questions?"

"We're trying to figure out what time the guy in your backyard was shot."

Mrs. Martin took a step back and pulled her robe tighter around her body. "Well, I had nothing to do with it! I have a gun, but it's for my protection. I didn't shoot anyone!"

"We know you didn't," Jeffrey said. "But we got here at seven-thirty and nothing has happened since then. So he must have been shot or dumped in your yard before we arrived. What time did you wake up today?"

The old woman squinted. "Who are you again?"

"It's me and Pablo!" Jeffrey shouted, his face flushing red. "You hired us to clean up your yard."

Pablo put a hand on Jeffrey's shoulder. "Mrs. Martin, we don't mean to scare you, but this is very serious. There's a man in your yard who's been shot. We're just trying to figure out what time that happened. If you had your music playing, the gunshots could have happened early this morning and you wouldn't have heard them."

"Nonsense," Mrs. Martin said. "If there were gunshots in my yard, I would hear them, music or no music. My hearing is sharp, very sharp." A phone rang from inside the house. "See? I can hear that just fine." She left the boys and went to answer the phone.

"She's deaf in one ear," Pablo whispered.

Jeffrey nodded.

Mrs. Martin returned and said, "That's my grandson. He wants to know what you boys want."

Jeffrey threw up his hands.

"We're here to clean up your yard," Pablo told her.

Jeffrey stepped closer to the door. "Don't you remember anything?"

The woman lifted a bony finger and shook it at Jeffrey's face. "I knew you were trouble the first time I saw you. I never should have let you onto my property. Now go home."

She took a step back and slammed the door closed. The boys heard the lock turn. Jeffrey turned to Pablo with a disbelieving look.

The police arrived and took statements from both boys and from Mrs. Martin. The boys learned that the wounded man's name was Kevin Wong. When the paramedics loaded the man into an ambulance, Jeffrey asked where they were taking him.

"L.A. County."

"Do you think he'll live?"

"I doubt it," was the grim reply.

Chapter Two

The emergency waiting room at the county hospital was filled to capacity. Babies bawled, children shrieked and scuffled, and adults argued with hospital attendants or with each other. Others, too tired to argue, sat slumped in their seats, immersed in their smart phones or sleeping.

Jeffrey and Pablo sat on hard plastic chairs with their backs to the wall, and observed the chaos around them. Their chairs were connected with metal brackets to a long line of other hard plastic chairs and all the seats were occupied.

Jeffrey glanced down the row of seats. A girl caught his eye and he peered at her from behind his glasses. She was one of only a handful of Asians in the room. She held a cell phone to her ear, listening intently and showing no emotion

Jeffrey nudged Pablo and nodded in the girl's direction. Pablo glanced down the row of seats and saw her. He whispered to Jeffrey, "Chinese?"

Jeffrey nodded.

"You think she's here for Kevin Wong?"

Jeffrey nodded again.

"Sister? Cousin?"

"Neither."

He saw Pablo's surprised reaction and tapped his own face, below the corner of his eye. "Remember this?"

"The three dots?"

"Right. The guy we found was a gang member. Now look at the way she's dressed."

Pablo looked again at the girl and observed her appearance. She looked to be their age, fifteen, perhaps a year older, with high cheekbones and a model's face. Her hair was straight and black. She wore heels, a short black skirt, and a red school sweater with the letter M sewn on its front. Nearly everyone else in the room sat slumped and stoop-shouldered, but the girl sat ramrod straight. She stood up, long-legged and lithe, and strode to the attendant's desk. The boys followed her with their eyes.

"Look at her whole demeanor," Jeffrey whispered, "the way she carries herself and her posture."

"She looks rich," Pablo said.

"She looks *very* rich."

The girl spoke briefly to the desk attendant, and then returned to her seat and went back to listening on her phone.

"She seems too sophisticated to be hanging out with gang members," Pablo whispered.

"Exactly."

"Either that or she hides it well."

"That's possible too," Jeffrey said. "But here's the thing, most families stay true to form. There might be a black sheep somewhere along the line, but that's rare. A girl who dresses and carries herself like this one does is not in the same league as a guy with a tattoo on his face."

"Then why is she here?" Pablo asked.

"That's what we'll have to find out."

The girl lifted a finger and brushed her eye.

"Is she crying?" Pablo asked.

"I don't know."

The girl stood up suddenly, pocketed her phone and headed for the exit. Jeffrey tapped Pablo on the arm. The two boys rose quietly and followed her. As they stepped into hospital hallway, the girl was twenty feet ahead of them.

She walked briskly, her heels clack-clacking down the tile floor of the hospital hallway.

The boys quickened their pace to keep up.

Approaching in the opposite direction, a hospital orderly pushed an elderly patient in a wheelchair. The girl stepped past them both and turned a corner.

The boys ran down the hall, stepped past the orderly and the patient in the wheelchair, and turned the same corner. They saw the girl push open an exit door, pause for a brief moment, and then step through. They ran to catch up.

Jeffrey stopped before the exit door, opened it quietly and slipped through. Pablo followed him. They were in a stairwell. The girl was one floor below them, her heels clattering loudly down the aluminum steps. The sound echoed off the walls.

Pablo started after her.

Jeffrey grabbed his arm. "She'll hear us," he whispered.

Pablo nodded.

The girl descended two more floors, pulled open a door on the landing, and stepped through. The door closed behind her and Jeffrey said, "Let's go!"

Their feet tapped lightly down the stairs. They reached the door the girl had opened and Jeffrey pulled. The door didn't budge.

"It's locked," Jeffery said.

"How come she opened it?"

Jeffrey shook his head. He studied the door. There was no keyhole in the doorknob and no way to unlock the door. He felt with his hand along the edges. The door suddenly swung open and the boys jumped back.

A young Asian male, dressed in a white coat and wearing a surgical mask on his face and a stethoscope around his neck, stepped into the stairwell. Jeffrey grabbed the door and held it open. Pablo stepped out of the man's way and said, "Sorry, doctor."

The surgical mask covered the young man's face, except for his eyes, which fixed the boys with an intense, burning stare. He regarded them both silently, then turned away and climbed the aluminum stairs. The boys looked at each other. Jeffrey nodded at the open door and he and Pablo stepped out of the stairwell. Ahead of them lay a long empty hall. The girl was nowhere in sight.

"We lost her," Pablo said.

Jeffrey blinked and stared absently down the hall.

"Did you hear me?" Pablo asked.

Jeffrey nodded. He took a few steps down the hall and Pablo followed.

"What is it, Jeffrey?"

Jeffrey stopped. "Did you notice anything unusual about that doctor we just saw?"

"He looked kind of young."

"Besides that."

"He had rattlesnake eyes."

"Good observation. He also wasn't wearing an identification badge. In California all doctors are required to wear identification badges."

"So what does that mean?"

"It means ..." Jeffrey paused and looked at his friend, "... he's probably not a doctor."

Pablo's eyes widened. He turned and bolted for the stairwell, Jeffrey right behind him. Pablo pushed open the exit door and looked up the stairwell. The man was gone. He started up the stairs, two at a time.

Jeffrey called to him from the open stairwell door, "Wait. We might get stuck in the stairwell again."

"He didn't."

"Maybe he knows something we don't."

"That's the whole point."

Jeffrey nodded and followed Pablo up the stairwell. They climbed three flights of stairs back to the floor where they came from and pulled on the door. It swung open easily.

Jeffrey stuck his fingers into the hollow slot in the door frame. "Look," he said, and pulled out a wad of paper.

"The girl must have put it there," Pablo said, "to keep the door from locking."

"Right," Jeffrey said. "We didn't notice it the first time. That's how she opened the door downstairs. She must have put something in there earlier, and then she propped this door open when we were following her, so that fake doctor could sneak up to this floor without being noticed."

"But why?"

Jeffrey threw the wad of paper on the floor and looked Pablo straight in the eye. "To finish the job."

Pablo's eyebrows arched high. "Come on," he shouted, and ran down the hall.

In the emergency waiting room, an enormous, round-faced black woman with eyes like a sick hound dog pressed against the front desk. Her arms shook like Jell-O as she waved them and spoke to the young black woman on duty. "I've been waitin' two hours to see a doctor. I can't wait no more."

The young woman seated behind the desk blinked behind her glasses and spoke with a Jamaican accent. "I understand."

"No, you don't understand. I'm sick, my feet hurt, and I need a doctor. I need a doctor to look at my feet."

"I'm sorry. We are very busy today."

"I'm busy too. I'm busy and I'm tired, so you call me a doctor right now."

Pablo sprinted into the room and scanned the area quickly. The girl and the Asian doctor from the stairwell were nowhere to be found. Jeffrey caught up with him and Pablo shook his head. "They're not here."

Jeffrey led the way to the front desk, stepping past the round-faced woman.

"Have you seen an Asian doctor?" he asked the attendant.

"Excuse me," cried the round-faced woman. "Excuse me, I'm talking here."

"Sorry, ma'am," Pablo said, "this is an emergency."

"I have my own emergency. I need someone to look at my feet."

The young woman behind the desk leaned toward Jeffrey, welcoming the distraction. "What did you say?"

"An Asian doctor," Jeffrey said. "Have you seen an Asian doctor?"

The young woman looked down at a list on her desk. "What is his name?"

"I don't know his name. He's just a doctor; an Asian man in a white coat, with a stethoscope around his neck."

The young woman leaned back in her chair. "An Asian man in a white coat?"

"That's right."

The round-faced woman leaned across Pablo and slapped Jeffrey on the shoulder. "Did you hear me, fat boy?"

"Call security," Jeffrey said to the attendant.

"Don't be calling security on me," the round-faced woman said. "I'll knock your lights out."

"It's not on you, lady," Pablo said.

The young woman behind the desk stared up at Jeffrey and blinked her eyes.

"Call security," Jeffrey said again, his voice louder and impatient.

Gunfire cracked from down the hall.

The round-faced woman shoved Pablo out of the way and ran for the main hallway.

In the waiting area, heads snapped, followed by screams. A swarm of shrieking humanity rose out of their seats and ran for the exit. The young woman attendant ducked under her desk.

Tables tipped in the waiting area. An old woman fell and was trampled over. The crowd barreled into Jeffrey, knocking him back. He clung to the attendant's desk for support. He heard screams and shouts and felt bodies bumping into his and rushing past.

A young Hispanic mother rose out of her seat, confused and frightened and clutching her newborn baby. The stampeding crowd bowled her over. She screamed as she hit the floor and her baby, wrapped in a pink blanket, spilled out of her hands.

Pablo saw the child and threw his body over hers as a shield. Hysterical men and women stomped over his back and legs as they raced for the exit.

More people came running from the hall where the shots were fired, wild-eyed and screaming. Pablo scooped up the baby, got his feet up under him, and scurried to Jeffrey's side. Jeffrey shielded them against the attendant's desk. Shrieking bodies flew past them.

Huddled against the desk, Pablo unfurled his arms. The baby stared up at him and blinked her big eyes.

Pablo looked down at the baby and smiled. The baby's mother crawled to him on her knees and stretched out her arms.

"Gracias! Gracias!"

Pablo handed her the baby and the young mother burst into tears.

Chapter Three

"So you found a body?"

"Yes, sir," Jeffrey replied. "Dead as a doornail or so we thought. When we checked his pulse, we found out he was still alive. That's when we called the police."

The two men seated across the table from him and Pablo were homicide detectives. Both men wore suits, both sported mustaches and both had carefully coifed short hair. Detective Wolfe was big and snarling. Detective Ratburn had a thin neck and small eyes that shifted from one boy to the other. They were seated in a makeshift interrogation room, down the hall from where Kevin Wong lay dead in his hospital bed.

Jeffrey repeated the same story he'd told the police officers who first arrived at Mrs. Martin's house. Then he told the two men about how he and Pablo had taken a bus to the hospital and how they had followed the girl from the waiting room down the hospital staircase. When he told them of the Asian doctor they saw and how the doors in the stairwell were stuffed with paper wads to keep them from locking, Detective Ratburn rolled back in his chair and snickered.

"Sounds like a comic book story," he said.

"Jeffrey doesn't read comic books," Pablo told him.

"But you do, don't you, boy?"

Pablo stared back at the man for a moment, and then lowered his eyes to the table.

Ratburn grinned and glanced at his partner, but Wolfe's eyes were fixed on Jeffrey.

"We didn't find any of the doors in the stairwell stuffed with paper wads to keep them from locking," Wolfe said.

"I told you," Jeffrey replied, "I threw the paper on the floor."

"We didn't find anything on the floor either."

Ratburn grinned wider. "Like I said, a comic book story."

Jeffrey felt his face flushing red. "It's not a comic book. It's what really happened."

Wolfe glanced at his notes on the table before him. "I understand you're both amateur detectives."

Jeffrey squirmed. He'd been questioned by the police before, but these two men had him on edge. "That's correct," he answered.

Pablo noticed Jeffrey's discomfort and sat straight up in his chair. "Actually, we're not amateurs."

"What was that?" Wolfe snapped.

"I said we're not amateurs. We got paid on our last case."

Wolfe's eyes narrowed. "Paid by whom?"

"Our teacher."

"Ha!" said Ratburn.

"How much did your teacher pay you?" Wolfe asked.

"A hundred dollars. Each."

"Ha!" said Ratburn.

Pablo shot the man an angry look.

Jeffrey slid deeper into his seat.

Wolfe rocked back in his chair and smiled wide. "Oh, yeah.... I heard about that. The great treasure hunting case."

"That's the one," Jeffrey muttered.

"And who's paying you on this case?"

"Nobody."

"I guess you don't have to get paid, since you found a treasure, right? How much was it worth?" Wolfe flipped through his notes. "Ah, here it is: two hundred million dollars. I suppose I wouldn't need to get paid either if I was as rich as both of you."

"We're not rich," Jeffrey said quietly.

"Not rich? How can you not be rich after you found a treasure worth two hundred million dollars?"

"You guys impounded it."

"*You* guys?"

"Not *you* guys," Jeffrey waved his hand to indicate the two men, "the police in Santa Barbara."

"So you got nothing?"

Jeffrey lowered his eyes. "No."

"Ha!" said Ratburn.

Pablo shot the man another angry look.

Wolfe turned to his partner. "Imagine that? Finding a treasure worth two hundred million dollars and not getting a single penny."

Ratburn chuckled.

Wolfe turned back to the boys. "It seems to me you should have learned something from such a stupid escapade."

"We did learn something," Jeffrey said.

"And what was that?"

"All that glitters is not gold."

Pablo laughed, drawing angry looks from both detectives.

Wolfe focused back on Jeffrey and narrowed his eyes. "Don't crack jokes at me, kid."

"It's not a joke," Jeffrey said.

"When I said you should have learned something, I meant you should have learned enough to mind your own business and keep police work to the professionals. I know all about your little treasure hunt. Or should I say *deadly* treasure hunt. Two suspects killed in a car accident."

"That's not our fault," Pablo said. "They were chasing us. They lost control of their car."

Wolfe slammed his fist down on the table. "I don't care whose fault it was! Or who was chasing who! The fact is they're dead and you're not! And now you're sticking your nose into a murder case, telling us how to do our jobs."

"We're not telling you how to do your jobs," Jeffrey said. "We're telling you what we saw. The girl we followed went down an emergency stairwell. Three floors down she opened a door on the landing, but when we came to the same door, it wouldn't open. A minute or two later, an Asian man in a white coat came through the same door and into the stairwell. Then he took the stairs going up. He was wearing a white coat like a doctor and a surgical mask, but he wasn't wearing an identification badge."

Jeffrey paused for a moment to make sure the detectives were following him. "Every door in that stairwell is locked from the inside. The girl stuffed something into the hollow part of each of the door frames to keep them from locking. That's how she was able to move from floor to floor, and that's how the man in the white coat was able to enter the emergency floor from the stairway without being seen. It's also how he made his escape."

"His escape?"

"Yes, he's the killer, and the girl is an accomplice."

"Whoa!" said Ratburn, pushing back from the table.

Wolfe licked his lips, leaned his bulky body over the table, and leveled an accusing finger at Jeffrey. "Now hold on second, you're saying this man you saw in the stairwell is the one who shot Kevin Wong in his hospital bed?"

"Isn't it obvious?"

Pablo looked proudly at Jeffrey, then back at the two policemen. Neither one was smiling.

"Now I know you're crazy," Wolfe said. He reached inside a manila folder on the table in front of him and pulled out a photograph of an Asian male wearing a white doctor's coat. He tossed the picture across the table to Jeffrey. "That's the man you saw in the stairwell."

Pablo stood up and leaned in over Jeffrey's shoulder. They both studied the picture. Pablo shook his head, and Jeffrey said, "No, that's not him."

"It *is* him," said Wolfe. He laid a pencil over the lower half of the man's face. "That's him wearing the surgical mask you described."

"No, it's not."

Wolfe lumbered to his feet, leaned over the table and jabbed the photograph with his meaty finger. "*That* is the man you saw in the hospital stairwell."

"It's not him," Jeffrey insisted. "The man we saw was Chinese, this man is Korean."

"*What?*"

Jeffrey pointed to the photograph. "This man is Korean."

Wolfe turned to his partner.

"His name is Doctor Sam Park," Ratburn said. "Korean."

Wolfe turned back to Jeffrey. "The man in that picture is the only Asian male doctor on staff at the county hospital, and he just so happened to be on duty this morning. We even saw him on the surveillance video, running away with the rest of the crowd. And at the time the shots were fired, he was in a room down the hall with a patient and the patient's family. Three witnesses all verifying his location, so you see, your theory is hogwash."

"It's not hogwash," Jeffrey said, "because this man is not the man we saw. What's more, the man we saw was younger than the man in this picture, and he was pretending to be a doctor, not a real doctor."

"Not a real doctor, huh? And you know this, because he wasn't wearing his identification badge?"

"That's right."

Wolfe leaned back in his chair. "You're the boy genius, right? The boy genius who finds a treasure worth two hundred million dollars, but isn't smart enough to keep any of it for himself."

"Ha!" said Ratburn.

"And what if I told you," said Wolfe, smiling now, "that we examined all of the surveillance video at the time of the shooting and immediately after, and we couldn't find a single Asian male, doctor or patient, anywhere, except for the man whose picture you have in front of you?"

"I'd say that when those bullets went off, it was a stampede. You had a hundred people fleeing the area all at once. An Asian man, including the killer, could have easily blended in and been hidden in that crowd. I know, because I was there."

"I was there too," said Pablo, "and I'd say the same thing."

Wolfe glowered at the two boys. "And what would you say if I told you that in all of our surveillance footage, we didn't see any males dressed in a white coat fleeing the scene, except for that man in the picture? You see, except for Doctor Park, the doctors on staff this morning were all female. No white coats, no stethoscopes, no other doctors."

"Obviously, he took those things off," Jeffrey said. "The white coat was just to get into the hospital and into the victim's room without suspicion. After he killed Kevin Wong, he took the white coat off and blended in with the mob. That white coat probably has blood on it and some gun residue. Did you check the closets and laundry baskets?"

The two detectives exchanged a quick look, and Jeffrey and Pablo both knew that they hadn't.

"Great imagination, kid," said Ratburn.

"It's not imagination," Jeffrey said. "And one more thing," he tapped the picture on the table in front of him. "You said you saw this man on the surveillance video running from the scene of the shooting. Was he wearing his identification badge? The man we saw in the stairwell was not wearing his badge. If you saw this man," he tapped the photo again, "wearing his identification badge, then it proves he wasn't the man we saw."

"Maybe he took his badge off," Ratburn said.

He unclipped his own badge from his chest, slipped it into his shirt pocket, and flashed a crooked smile.

"Why would he do that?" Jeffrey asked. "It's illegal, isn't it? For him to take his badge off isn't logical. And it proves my theory is correct."

"It doesn't prove anything," Wolfe said. "Now I've had just about enough from both of you." He pointed at the picture in front of Jeffrey. "That's the man you saw in the hospital stairway."

"No, it's not," Pablo protested.

"Shut up! It *is* him. We even talked to him. He even said he passed both of you in the stairwell."

"That's impossible!" Pablo said.

"Shut up," said Ratburn.

"It's him," Wolfe insisted. "He confirmed it, and we accepted it. Now get out of here, both of you. And you better hope I never run across either of your names or faces ever again."

Jeffrey sat staring at the two police detectives.

Pablo shook his head. "This is crazy."

Wolfe jerked his thumb towards the door. "Out."

Jeffrey and Pablo rose shakily out of their chairs and headed for the door.

"Go read some more comic books," Ratburn said.

Pablo stopped in the doorway and glared at the grinning man. Jeffrey took Pablo by the sleeve and pulled him out of the room.

Chapter Four

"I thought we were on the same side," Pablo said.

"Apparently not," Jeffrey replied.

The two boys sat slumped on the curb of a circular driveway in front of the hospital, their jacket collars pulled up high. The sun hung bright overhead, but the air was cold and harsh and the wind rustled their hair. An endless parade of cars and ambulances drove past, unloaded their passengers at the hospital entrance, and drove on.

"It takes a certain amount of intelligence to become a homicide detective," Jeffrey said. "But those two guys seemed incapable of any kind of logical thought."

"You would think they'd be interested in what we had to say."

"You would think. Anyway, it confirms my suspicions."

"What suspicions?"

"People are idiots."

Pablo laughed.

"I'm serious," Jeffrey said.

"I know you are, that's what's so funny." Pablo thought for a moment and added, "I think that guy we found, Kevin Wong, was a stool pigeon."

Jeffrey turned to him and Pablo continued: "Why else would the people who killed him go out of their way to make sure he was dead?"

"I thought about that," Jeffrey said. "To a criminal, there's nothing worse than a rat. But I think there might be something more here."

"Keep talking."

"Kevin Wong was shot up pretty bad when we found him," Jeffrey said. "It seems like that would be payback enough, even for a stool pigeon. Plus, there was no guarantee he was going to live. The paramedics even told us they doubted he would live."

"I remember that."

"So the guy's shot up, probably going to die, but the killer came here anyway, taking a huge risk, just to make sure he was dead. That doesn't make sense if the guy was just a stool pigeon."

"Then why, Jeffrey?"

"Why kill him?"

"Yeah, why take the risk, like you said? Unless ..."

"Unless what?"

"Unless somebody wanted to shut him up?"

Jeffrey grinned. "Now you're thinking like a detective. Dead men tell no tales, and neither will this one. Kevin Wong knew something and the killer had to finish him off to make sure he wouldn't talk."

"Talk about what?"

Jeffrey paused and looked at his friend. "A crime bigger than murder."

"Whoa! But what could be bigger than murder?"

"That's what we'll have to figure out."

Pablo sat up straight. "Are we on a new case?"

A uniformed security guard, tight-faced and beady-eyed, walked past, eyeing them. Pablo waited for the man to pass, and then lowered his voice to a whisper. "Are we on a new case?"

Jeffrey nodded. "Pablo, the case has officially begun. Only this one could be dangerous."

"Don't worry about me," Pablo said. "Danger is my middle name."

"Then our first job is to figure out the motive for this killing."

"A crime bigger than murder, you said."

"That's right. Now obviously there's no crime bigger than murder, but we have to think the way a criminal thinks. A criminal who's desperate enough will kill for a dollar, or even less. To them, a human life means nothing. For Kevin Wong's killer to sneak in here disguised as a doctor, with all the risks involved, just to make sure he wouldn't talk, seems to indicate a much bigger crime is at stake. I'm guessing it's a crime worth millions."

"What about the girl? She looked like she came from money."

"You're right. Kevin Wong was a lowlife gang member with tattoos on his face, but she wasn't like that at all. She makes the whole case even more of a mystery."

Pablo pointed with his thumb at the hospital behind them. "Should we go back and tell those cops all this?"

"Do you think they'd listen?"

Pablo thought for a moment. "No."

"Then what's the point? We're better off investigating ourselves."

Jeffrey thought back to the two homicide detectives at the hospital and frowned. They made him feel small and he wondered if maybe they were right and he was wrong. He wished he could have answered them more intelligently and presented his argument more convincingly.

Something else was bothering him and he turned to Pablo. "You saved that kid's life back at the hospital."

Pablo shrugged. "Somebody had to do it."

"But weren't you scared? You could have been killed."

"I wasn't really thinking. I just saw that mob coming and I knew they would have trampled that baby if I didn't do something."

Jeffrey lowered his eyes and studied the pavement between his feet. "I don't know if I could do that," he said quietly. "I'd be too scared."

"It's like what they say about life rafts," Pablo explained, "women and children first. As men, we have a responsibility to protect the weak and to do what's right."

Jeffrey nodded, but kept his eyes down. Sure, Pablo was a man. At fifteen, he was broad-shouldered, athletic, and girls liked him. As for himself, Jeffrey didn't know if he'd ever be a man, no matter how old he got.

"If you and your parents were on a sinking ship," Pablo said, "and there were only two lifejackets, would you give them both to your parents, or would you keep one for yourself?"

Jeffrey thought for a long moment.

"Well," he said, "I'm not a very good swimmer."

"Aw, Jeffrey."

"I like to think I would give the life jackets to my parents, but I don't know if I actually would. Honestly, Pablo, I don't know if I could sacrifice my life for anyone, no matter who it was."

Pablo gave his friend a pat on the back. "Well, I trust you. If I hadn't been there today, you would have saved that baby."

Jeffrey wasn't so sure. "Maybe you trust me," he said, "but I don't know if I trust myself."

"I mean, what's the point of living," he heard Pablo say, "what's the point of being a man if we're not willing to sacrifice ourselves to protect the people around us?"

Jeffrey sagged within himself. A line he'd once read flashed in his mind: *Cowards die many times before their deaths; The valiant never taste of death but once.*

"Right?" Pablo said.

"Right," Jeffrey replied, but his tone held no meaning. He turned to Pablo. "Isn't there anything you're afraid of?"

Pablo laughed. "Your dad."

He'd meant it as a joke, but Jeffrey wasn't smiling. His eyes were fixed on a familiar car as it turned, tires screaming, from the street onto the hospital's circular driveway. Jeffrey's eyes went to the driver and his father's face came into focus.

"Uh-oh," Pablo said. "He looks mad."

The car spun around the driveway to where the boys sat and screeched to a stop. Jeffrey and Pablo rose uneasily to their feet.

Mr. Jones popped his car door open and started to climb out.

"Do we tell him about the case?" Pablo whispered.

Jeffrey shook his head.

Jeffrey's father slammed the car door shut, stalked his way around the rear of the car to the curb, and stood with his arms outstretched and his palms up, staring at Jeffrey.

"Well?" he said.

"Well what?"

"Well, what kind of a mess are you in now?"

"I'm not in a mess. The guy who got shot, he's in a mess."

"Don't get smart with me, kid. You tell me you're going out to rake leaves and this is what happens? You get yourself involved in a shooting?"

"We're not *involved*," Jeffrey said. "We're witnesses."

"It's like this, Mr. Jones," said Pablo, and he told Jeffrey's father everything that occurred that morning at Mrs. Martin's backyard and at the hospital.

"Hold on a second," said Mr. Jones. "You called the cops ... they took the guy away in an ambulance ... Why did you have to follow them to the hospital?"

Jeffrey cleared his throat. "Ancient Chinese saying: When you save a man's life, you become responsible for him."

Pablo turned to his friend. "Did you make that up?"

Jeffrey shrugged.

"Enough with the second-rate Confucius," said Jeffrey's father. "Get in the car." He stepped back around to the driver's side of his vehicle.

"Can we give Pablo a ride home?" Jeffrey asked.

Mr. Jones didn't respond. He opened the driver's side door, slid in behind the wheel, and slammed the car door closed.

Pablo turned to Jeffrey with an uneasy look. Jeffrey motioned at him to take the back seat. Pablo hesitated and Jeffrey motioned again. The boys stepped to the car. Jeffrey opened the front passenger door, plopped down on the leather car seat and closed the car door. Pablo stood outside the backseat door. Jeffrey's father sat behind the wheel, his jaw clenched, staring straight ahead.

"Can we give Pablo a ride?" Jeffrey said.

He heard a click as his father unlocked the back seat door. Pablo climbed inside.

Mr. Jones turned the ignition and pulled the car forward along the hospital's circular driveway.

"Witnesses, huh?" He shook his head. They passed an ambulance, parked alongside the curb, with its back door open. A pair of EMS workers unloaded a woman in a stretcher from the back of the ambulance.

"Witnesses get killed, too, you know."

"I don't think the killer knows who we are," Jeffrey said.

Jeffrey's father shot him a look. "You better hope not, boy."

Ahead of them, a red sports car, driven by a blond woman in a fur coat, pulled away from the curb and cut directly in front of them. Mr. Jones slammed the brakes with his foot, and Jeffrey and Pablo lurched forward against their seat belts.

Mr. Jones jammed the car horn with the palm of his hand. The driver of the car in front of them thrust her arm out the window and made an obscene gesture with her fingers.

Mr. Jones rolled down his window. "Learn how to drive!" he shouted.

The driver in front of them made the same obscene gesture, accelerated, and drove off.

Mr. Jones shook his head. "No one in this city knows how to drive."

He eased the car forward. "I have things to do at home, you know. I'm not supposed to be here."

"Sorry," Jeffrey said.

"You're a lightning rod for trouble, you know that?"

Jeffrey shrank into the leather car seat.

Mr. Jones glanced up at the rear view mirror. "Did you know that, Pablo? This kid's a lightning rod for trouble. One of these days he's going to get you killed."

Pablo laughed nervously.

"I'm not joking. You or someone else, he's going to get them killed."

"That's not going to happen," Jeffrey said quietly.

His father shot him a look. "Oh, no? What makes you so sure?"

"Because I'm careful."

"Careful doesn't mean squat. There's always the unexpected. Remember that."

"The unexpected," Jeffrey repeated.

"That's right." Mr. Jones pulled the car out of the hospital driveway and onto the street. "Old Loretta Martin called me, screaming up a storm in German. And then her grandson called me, screaming up a storm in English. You scared that poor woman half to death."

"I was trying to save a guy's life," Jeffrey said.

"I don't care what you were trying to do. It doesn't give you the right to run roughshod over other people, especially an old woman like that."

Jeffrey turned to his father with a look of disbelief. "What's more important, saving a man's life, or some old lady's feelings?"

"Now you listen to me," his father responded. "I've just about had it with that attitude."

"What attitude?"

"*Your* attitude."

Jeffrey turned to Pablo in the back seat for help.

His father noticed and snapped, "You leave Pablo out of this."

Jeffrey turned to the side and stared out the car window. "I don't know what you mean."

"You know exactly what I mean," his father said, "so don't pretend like you don't. Your attitude is sickening. You think you're the smartest person in the world and everyone else around you is an idiot.

"They are idiots."

Mr. Jones swung the steering wheel to the side and slammed the brakes. The boys jerked forward in their seats as the car skidded to a stop along the curb.

Mr. Jones turned to Jeffrey. "Now you listen and listen good: You're fifteen-years-old. And contrary to what goes on in that mind of yours, you're not the smartest person in the world."

"I never said I was."

"You don't have to say it. It's written all over your face. You have a sense of superiority that oozes out of every pore in your body. You act like you're some kind of king, lording over the world and surrounded by peasants. Like the way you treated Mrs. Martin this morning." He glanced at Pablo in the rearview mirror. "Am I right, Pablo?"

Pablo squirmed in his seat.

Mr. Jones turned back to Jeffrey. "It's not your job to solve the world's crimes."

"I know it's not my job, but shouldn't we at least try to help people when we can?"

"No."

Jeffrey sat up. "If I had my own phone, I could have called the police myself. I wouldn't have to bother people like Mrs. Martin."

"Forget it."

"I'm serious."

"So am I. We've been over this before. You're not getting a phone until you're over sixteen. *Well* over sixteen."

"That's forever," Jeffrey protested.

"Forever and a dream," his father said, and he pulled the car back into traffic.

Chapter Five

"Idiots!" Pablo said. He stared down at the wild grilled salmon and bright green broccoli on his dinner plate.

"Who you calling an idiot, boy?" asked his father. "Those are policemen you're talking about."

They sat at the dinner table with Pablo's mother and his nine-year-old sister, Maria.

"I'm not saying *all* policemen are idiots, just those two guys who questioned me and Jeffrey."

"Why? Because they told you to mind your own business?"

"Basically, yeah."

Mr. Reyes snorted.

"I'm just glad you're alive," said Mrs. Reyes.

"Me too," said Pablo.

"Me three," said Maria, and smiled.

Mrs. Reyes rose out of her seat and carried her empty plate to the sink.

"Sit down, Veronica," said her husband, but she pretended not to hear him. She had read in one of her style magazines that it was a good habit to leave the table before you were full, so she served herself small portions of food and was always the first in the family to finish eating. She turned on the hot water in the sink and waited for it to warm.

Mr. Reyes speared a sliver of salmon with his fork. "Let me tell you something," he told Pablo, "grown men don't like kids telling them how to do their jobs." He popped the fish in his mouth and chewed.

"We weren't telling them how to do their jobs."

"You weren't?"

"Well, maybe just a little."

"You see!"

"But that's not the point."

"Then what is?"

Pablo gave his father an exasperated look. "The point is Jeffrey told them exactly how the murder happened and they wouldn't listen. It was like they didn't even want to hear it."

"Jeffrey's smart," said Mrs. Reyes. She closed the drain in the sink as the hot water ran, reached for a container of liquid soap, and squirted it into the running water.

Mr. Reyes nodded. "Jeffrey *is* smart, I'll give him that. But I don't know if he's smarter than a pair of homicide detectives."

"I think he is," said Mrs. Reyes.

"Me too," said Maria.

Mr. Reyes glanced at Maria, then at his wife, and then back at Pablo. "Well, if the police acted that way, I'm sure they have their reasons."

"Stupid reasons," Pablo said.

Mr. Reyes set his fork down on his plate and rubbed his chin. "I have to admit, I'm still mad at those Santa Barbara police for impounding our treasure."

"You mean *our* treasure," Pablo said. "Mine and Jeffrey's. We're the ones who found it."

Mr. Reyes feigned indignation. "What, and leave me out? You wouldn't do that to your own father, would you?"

Pablo squirmed.

Mr. Reyes went on. "You'd throw your old man a bone, wouldn't you? Some precious gold coins, or a magic ruby or two?"

"Maybe," Pablo said.

"*Maybe?* What's this *maybe*?" Mr. Reyes turned to his wife as she dipped her plate into the sudsy water in the sink. "Did you hear what this one said?"

"Would you give me some of your treasure, Pablo?" Mrs. Reyes asked, without turning around.

"Sure, Mom. I'd give you something. Some gold coins or some magic rubies or something. I'm just not sure about Dad."

"Oh, so that's the way it is, huh?" said Mr. Reyes, and he leapt out of his chair and caught Pablo in a playful headlock. Pablo grabbed at his father's arm and the two of them banged into the dinner table. Plates and silverware rattled.

"Don't!" Mrs. Reyes shrieked.

"I gotcha now," Mr. Reyes panted, his arm locked around Pablo's head, "I gotcha now."

Maria hollered, "Headlock! Headlock!"

"Not in the house," Mrs. Reyes shouted.

Pablo tried to stand. His father dragged him by the head across the kitchen. "Come on, show me something," his father grunted. He and Pablo stumbled out of the kitchen and into the living room. Maria sprang out of her chair and followed them.

"Stop it!" Mrs. Reyes called from the kitchen.

Mr. Reyes tightened his grip around Pablo's neck and they wrestled across the living room, bumping into the coffee table and brushing against the Christmas tree. The tree tilted. Ornaments fell to the floor.

"Get him, Maria," Pablo shouted.

Maria screamed and leapt onto her father's back.

"Two against one, no fair!" Mr. Reyes said.

Mrs. Reyes stepped into the living room, waving a soapy plate in her hand. "Stop it, before you break something!"

Mr. Reyes kept one arm around Pablo's neck and reached over his shoulder for Maria with the other. He pulled Maria over his back and she landed on the couch with a shriek.

Mrs. Reyes stomped her foot. "I said stop!"

Mr. Reyes twisted Pablo's body, both of them bent at the waist, and pulled his arm tighter around the boy's neck. "Some street punk has a hold of you and he's gonna choke you out. What are you gonna do, huh? What are you gonna do?"

Pablo reached down with both hands and grabbed his father's ankle. He lifted his father's ankle off the floor and shoved his weight against his father's bulk. The two of them fell to the floor.

The fall broke his father's grip and they tousled on the floor before his father said, "Alright, alright, that's enough."

Maria sat up on the couch and clapped her hands.

Pablo and his father lay on the floor, panting and looking up at the ceiling. "You know, you're pretty tough when you want to be," his father said.

Mrs. Reyes waved the plate in her hand. "How many times have I told you, not in the house?"

Mr. Reyes leaned up on an elbow to look at her.

"That's self-defense, woman. He might need that someday."

Mrs. Reyes turned and started out of the room. "This is a house, not a barn," she said over her shoulder and entered the kitchen.

"We didn't break anything," called Mr. Reyes from the living room.

"Not *this* time."

"You're the one who needs to be careful."

"Don't tell me to be careful," said Mrs. Reyes, and she crossed the kitchen to the sink. "I'm the only careful person in this house."

The soapy plate squirted out of her hand. "Aye!" she cried as the plate hit the tile floor and splinters of porcelain flew in every direction.

From the living room, three voices burst out laughing.

Chapter Six

"I can't believe you're in trouble again, Jeffrey."

Jeffrey stared at his mother, seated across from him at the kitchen table. His father sat hunched at the head of the table, looking like he'd had enough for one day. Steaming bowls of soup sat on the table before each of them, and the scent of chicken, onions and carrots filled the room.

"I'm not in trouble," Jeffrey said. "I'm a witness. You act like I'm the one who committed murder."

"Murder!" cried his mother.

"That's what it is," Jeffrey said, his voice rising.

Mrs. Jones turned to her husband, who merely shrugged.

"I told him he was a lightning rod for trouble," said Mr. Jones. He blew softly on the steam rising from his soup bowl, dispersing it to the sides, and sending little ripples across the liquid surface.

Mrs. Jones stirred her soup with a spoon. "I just wish we could have a normal life."

"What's normal?" Jeffrey asked.

"I'll tell you what's normal," his mother said. "It's not getting phone calls from the police telling us you're in trouble."

"I just told you I'm not in trouble."

"When we get phone calls about you from the police," his mother said, "you're in trouble." She lifted a spoonful of soup to her lips, blew on it, and swallowed it down.

"You're the one who suggested we help clean Mrs. Martin's yard."

Jeffrey's mother looked up to see both Jeffrey and Mr. Jones looking at her and she blushed. "I did that so you could earn some money and to help Mrs. Martin. She can't clean that whole yard by herself."

"I earned money, all right," Jeffrey said. "In all the commotion we never finished and I never got paid."

"Well, whose fault is that?" Mrs. Jones turned to her husband. "Did you tell him that Mrs. Martin called here?"

Mr. Jones nodded. "I told him."

"How could you, Jeffrey?" his mother said. "You frightened that poor woman to her wit's end. You know what it's called when you think only about yourself? It's called being selfish. *Very* selfish."

Jeffrey scowled.

His mother shook her head. "Poor Mrs. Martin."

"Maybe she shot the guy," said Mr. Jones, and took a loud slurp of soup.

Mrs. Jones turned to him. "Brad!"

Mr. Jones shrugged. "I'm just thinking like Jeffrey does. I'm applying deductive reasoning. It is possible that Mrs. Martin is the killer, isn't it, Jeffrey?"

"Sure. Anything's possible." Jeffrey corralled a large chunk of chicken, spooned it, and chewed. Out of the side of his mouth, he added, "I wouldn't put it past her, the old hag."

Mrs. Jones dropped her spoon. It hit her bowl with a clang and sent soup splashing up and across the table.

Jeffrey leaned back, aghast. "Mom!"

"How can you say that?" his mother cried.

"Say what?"

"What you just said!"

"What did I say?"

"You know what you said!" She turned to her husband. "Brad?"

Without looking up, Mr. Jones took a loud slurp of soup. "Apologize to your mother," he said.

"Apologize for what?" Jeffrey demanded.

Mr. Jones looked at his wife. "Apologize for what?"

"For insulting me," she said.

"For insulting her," said Mr. Jones, and he made a motion with his spoon from Jeffrey to Mrs. Jones.

"I didn't insult her. I was talking about that old hag Mrs. Martin."

"You did it again!" said Mrs. Jones.

"Did *what?*"

"Called me an old hag!"

"I'm not talking about *you.*"

"Stop it," Mrs. Jones shrieked. Jeffrey and his father both looked at her. "I'm going to be old someday, Jeffrey," she cried. "Are you going to talk about me like that?"

"No, Mom. I didn't mean you. I'm sorry."

His mother put her elbows on the table, covered her face with her hands and began to weep.

Mr. Jones glowered at Jeffrey from the head of the table. "Now you see what you did?"

"You told me to apologize, I apologized," Jeffrey said.

Mrs. Jones sobbed loudly. "I'm going to be an old hag!"

Jeffrey pushed back from the table. The tips of his chair legs screeched against the tile floor. His mother looked up through tear-streaked eyes. "Where are you going?"

Jeffrey stood up. "The living room."

"Sit down, finish your dinner."

"I'll finish it later," Jeffrey said.

"He'll finish it later," Mr. Jones said.

"It'll be cold," said his mother.

"I don't care," Jeffrey said.

"He doesn't care," Mr. Jones said.

Jeffrey stepped around the kitchen table.

His mother reached out for him. "Jeffrey, sit down."

"Let him go," said his father.

"I want him to finish his dinner."

"He'll finish it later."

Jeffrey stepped out of the room and into the hall. He heard his mother's voice behind him: "Why do we have to fight like this?"

"It's all over," his father said.

"No, it's not all over, it's never over, and the whole thing is your fault, Brad."

"*My* fault?"

"You're the one who said Mrs. Martin might be a murderer."

Jeffrey tuned them out and continued down the hall.

It was cool and dark in the living room. Tiny bulbs of blue and red light blinked from the Christmas tree in the corner. Jeffrey slumped into the big easy chair that his father called his own. He felt the tiredness of the day's events pulling on him like a weight and he sank deeper into the smooth contours of the chair. The bright scent of candy canes and peppermint licorice that decorated the Christmas tree tickled his nose.

His parents' voices drifted in from the kitchen. They were still arguing. Jeffrey sighed and focused his hearing on the sound of bubbling water from the aquarium atop the table next to him. Goldfish darted about in the water, zipping from one end of the lighted tank to the other.

The shrill kitchen voices soon gave way to the gurgling water of the aquarium and Jeffrey could think again. He leaned his head back against the soft leather of the chair and closed his eyes. Light from the aquarium cast an eerie glow over his face.

He thought of the shooting at the hospital and the girl that he and Pablo followed down the emergency staircase. Who was she, and what was her connection to the murder?

He had to find out.

Chapter Seven – 14 Days Before Christmas

Jeffrey's breath frosted in the forty-degree air. "Tell me what that nurse said again."

He and Pablo stood hunched against the cold on a sidewalk across the street from a high school in Monterey Park.

Pablo pulled his jacket collar up higher over his neck. "You know that squinty look she gets in her eye? She gave me that look. Then she goes, 'Mr. Reyes, I find it hard to believe that you and Jeffrey Jones both come to me ill on the same afternoon.' So I kind of swooned a little, and I made my voice sound all scratchy, and I'm like, 'I don't know anything about Jeffrey, but I think I'm going to throw up…. I think I'm going to throw up on you, Mrs. Stockton.' I never saw a person reach for a pen so fast in my life. She signed my sick excuse note, threw it across the desk at me, and yelled, 'Get out!' "

Jeffrey roared with laughter. Pablo joined him and shouted, "At least I didn't have to puke on her desk!"

When their laughter died down, Pablo said, "Are you sure this is the right school?"

Jeffrey reached in his jacket pocket and pulled out a crumpled sheet of paper. The wind rattled the paper as Jeffrey unfolded it and showed it to Pablo. "This is what I found on the internet." He pointed to the paper which featured a picture of a red sweater with the letter M sewn on it. "Recognize it?"

"Yeah," said Pablo, "it's the same sweater the girl at the hospital was wearing."

Jeffrey pointed across the street to the high school. A sign in front of the school read: Proud Home of the Monterey Park Mountaineers. The letter M in the words Monterey and Mountaineers was styled the same as the letter M on the sweater.

"Looks like a match," said Pablo. "But why would she wear a school sweater if she was out to commit a crime?"

"Ah, Detective Reyes, what does your deductive reasoning tell you?"

"Well, it's pretty stupid," Pablo said. "Either she wanted to get caught, or she made a really stupid mistake."

"Good reasoning. Of course, there's one other possibility." Jeffrey paused for a moment and added, "An unconscious cry for help."

The school bell rang across the street. Seconds later, students poured out the front and side doors of the building. The air filled with laughter, voices and shouts.

"They're all Asian," Pablo said.

Jeffrey nodded. "Chinese." His eyes scanned the crowd. "Remember what she looks like?"

"I think so," Pablo said. He pointed. "There! No wait ... False alarm."

A dozen students crossed the street, headed in the direction of the two boys. They gave Jeffrey and Pablo curious looks.

"They're wondering what we're doing here," Pablo said.

"Right. Come on." Jeffrey started across the street, headed towards the school. Pablo walked alongside of him.

A throng of students milled in front of the school, lighting up cigarettes and chattering on their phones. Jeffrey and Pablo ambled through their mist, drawing strange looks. Pablo grabbed Jeffrey's arm and nodded towards the school entrance. "Is that her?"

A Chinese girl strode deliberately down the front walk, carrying a purse, but no books. Jeffrey studied her. She had the same high cheekbones and model-like face as the girl he remembered from the hospital, with straight black hair, parted in the middle. Her purple lipstick matched the purple on her nails, and despite the chilly weather, she wore a short purple skirt, heels, and a tiny jacket.

"That's her," Jeffrey said.

The girl lifted a phone to her ear.

"She's always on that phone," Pablo said.

Jeffrey nodded. "It's a sign of low intelligence."

"It is?"

"To me, it is."

"To you, everything's a sign of low intelligence."

"Not everything, just most things. Now if she was reading, instead of talking, I'd judge it as a sign of high intelligence. But that's not why we're here. Come on."

The girl strode to the sidewalk. She put her phone in her purse and walked alone away from the school. The boys followed her.

Pablo spoke quietly. "I'd say anyone involved in murder is a person of low intelligence. No matter how clever they think they are."

"I'd say you're right," Jeffrey answered back.

The girl turned a corner. The boys followed. The girl quickened her pace, her short skirt swishing behind her.

"Did she see us?" Pablo asked.

Jeffrey shook his head. "She couldn't have seen us."

The girl stepped into a small corner market and the boys froze.

"Do we go in?" Pablo said.

Jeffrey shook his head.

"What if she slips out the back?"

Jeffrey's eyebrows went up and he looked at his friend.

Pablo tapped Jeffrey on the arm. "I'll cover it." In an instant, he was running to the back of the market.

Jeffrey positioned himself behind a lamppost and waited. Minutes ticked off. He started towards the front door of the market when he heard Pablo's whistle. He ran to the alley behind the market.

Pablo was waiting behind a dumpster. The girl was walking quickly down the litter-strewn alley, her heels clacking against the pavement.

"She didn't see me," Pablo said, "but she might have heard me whistle."

Jeffrey frowned. "Why is she going out the back door? She couldn't possibly have known we were following her."

"I don't know, but we better hurry or we'll lose her."

They followed her down the alley. The girl pulled a phone from her purse and dialed a number.

"She's on her phone again," Pablo said.

The girl reached the end of the alley and turned left, out of sight of the two boys. Jeffrey and Pablo broke into a run and emerged at the end of the alley. The girl was nowhere in sight.

"I don't believe it," Pablo said. "We lost her again."

A black sedan drove slowly past them, an elderly Asian man behind the wheel. The boys looked at the car, but saw no passengers. Jeffrey trained his eyes on the back of the car. The license plate was missing.

"This is insane," Pablo said. "It's like we're in a foreign country."

Inside the sedan, the elderly driver glanced up at the rear view mirror, and saw Jeffrey and Pablo standing at the end of the alley. He turned the car down a side street.

From the back seat came the sound of leather crunching. The girl, who had been lying on the back seat, hidden from view, sat up. She lifted her phone to her ear, and spoke in Chinese.

The boys began the long walk back to the bus stop, where they'd arrived.

"So much for that," Pablo said.

"We know where to find her," Jeffrey said.

"Yeah, but we can't leave school early like this again. This was our one chance to see where she lives or where she hangs out."

They crossed the street and walked past the high school. It was deserted now and the sidewalk was clear. They heard tires screech behind them and turned to see a black Mercedes skidding to a stop across the street. Jeffrey and Pablo wrinkled their noses at the smell of burnt rubber.

The doors to the Mercedes popped open and three Chinese teenagers piled out. They were older boys, dressed all in black. The two passengers crossed the street, headed towards Jeffrey and Pablo. The driver opened the trunk of the car, removed a baseball bat, and trotted to catch up with them.

The tallest of the three Chinese was the meanest-looking boy Jeffrey had ever seen, with a flat face, gaping pockmarks on his cheeks, and a crooked nose that looked like it had been broken more than once. He appeared to be the leader and he walked straight up to Jeffrey. "What are you doing here?"

"Nothing," Jeffrey said.

"You were following a lady."

The driver planted himself in front of Pablo. He was shorter than the others with a scar on his cheek. Pablo eyed him. The boy sneered and choked up on the bat.

Jeffrey recoiled inwardly at the sight of the leader standing in front of him. Something about the boy's ugliness seemed familiar to him, but before he could place it, the third boy, sporting a red headband, flanked out to the leader's side. "Man, you're in the wrong neighborhood," he said.

Jeffrey turned to the voice, and the leader struck. His fist hit Jeffrey flush on the cheek, knocking his glasses loose. Jeffrey dropped to the pavement. Above the pounding in his head he heard shouts and the sound of feet rushing in. He curled up and covered his face as feet kicked sharply at his ribs and stomped on his head and shoulders.

The driver swung the bat at Pablo's head, missed, and swung again. The bat whistled past Pablo's head and he lunged in. He grabbed the bat close to the knob with his right hand, and smashed his left fist into the driver's face. Blood spurted from the driver's nose and he yelped like a wounded pup.

Pablo twisted the bat and wrestled it free. He swung at the driver. The driver covered his head and the bat cracked him across the shoulder. The driver screamed and staggered back.

Pablo turned to the two boys stomping on Jeffrey and swung the bat at the first body in sight. The boy with the red headband put up his forearm just as the bat arrived and Pablo heard the crack of the wooden bat against bone. The boy screamed an obscenity and jumped back, along with the leader.

The leader lunged as if to charge. Pablo swung the bat at his head and the older boy jumped back.

"You come any closer and I'll bash your head in!" Pablo shouted.

The boy with the red headband gripped his wounded forearm and nodded at the driver. "Get your bat, man."

"You get it," the driver said. Blood poured from his nose and he looked ready to cry. He leaned his head back and inhaled a string of blood back into his nostrils.

Jeffrey lay on the concrete pavement, groaning.

"Jeffrey, get up," Pablo said, standing poised with the bat and keeping his eyes on the three boys in front of him.

Jeffrey groped for his glasses.

"Come on, Jeffrey," Pablo said.

Jeffrey found his glasses and put them on. The left corner hinge was broken.

The leader grinned. He pulled a twenty dollar bill from his pants pocket, wadded it into a hard ball, and threw it at Jeffrey. The projectile hit Jeffrey in the head and bounced off.

"Get your glasses fixed, fat boy," the leader said, almost laughing. He turned to Pablo, leveled a threatening gaze, and said, "We'll see you again." Then he waved his friends back to the Mercedes.

Chapter Eight - 12 Days Before Christmas

"Don't feel bad," Pablo said, "when I watch old movies, the detective always gets beat up."

Jeffrey groaned. A large purple welt covered his left cheek. It swelled up monstrously and made his eye look like a slit. The area underneath his eye was black. His glasses sat crooked on his nose with the left hinge held together by scotch tape. His arms were covered with purple bruises, and his ribs ached with every breath he took.

He and Pablo slid their plastic kitchen trays slowly over the stainless steel rail of the cafeteria breakfast line. A single file line of freshmen students trailed dutifully behind them, not daring to cut ahead of the two boys who were sophomores and a grade older than them.

The kitchen smelled of strawberries, cinnamon rolls, and fresh eggs scrambled in butter, but Jeffrey took no pleasure. Every muscle and tendon in his body screamed in pain.

Pablo stopped and picked up a white plastic knife from his tray. "I saw this one movie where a guy pulls a knife and sticks it up the detective's nose. The guy says, 'You're a nosy fellow. You know what happens to nosy fellows? They lose their noses.' Then they cut open his nose," Pablo flicked the little plastic knife, "and blood spurts everywhere."

Jeffrey frowned. "Did you have to tell me that?"

"Now you don't have to see it."

Standing behind a cash register at the far end of the line, a stout woman with heavy eyebrows, a pin in her nose, and orange-dyed hair, cut short as a boy's, called to them in a raspy voice, "Move it along back there."

"We're moving along," Pablo called back.

"Then move faster. You're clogging up my kitchen." Her grubby fingers popped the tab on a can of diet soda. She took a good pull and set the soda can next to the cash register.

Pablo dropped the plastic knife back on his tray. "It's *her* kitchen now." He and Jeffrey shuffled their trays down the line, followed by the younger students.

"What did your dad say?" Pablo asked.

"I told him I got in a fight. He wants me to take boxing lessons."

"I'll do it if you do," Pablo said.

Jeffrey grunted. "Surprisingly, he didn't yell. I thought for sure he'd yell at me."

"Did you tell him about the case?"

Jeffrey shook his head. "Then he really would've yelled. He did say I was selfish. So did my mom. Everyone I know tells me I'm selfish."

"Well you are selfish."

Jeffrey bristled and his voice rose an octave. "But I'm selfish for good reasons. We tried to save a guy's life."

The cashier glowered at them. "Move it along back there."

Jeffrey shot the woman an angry look. He slid his tray down the line. Pablo followed. The line of freshmen students followed them both.

Pablo had already eaten breakfast at home. He skipped ahead of Jeffrey, grabbed a banana from a selection of fruit, intending to eat it later, and placed it on his tray.

Jeffrey hadn't eaten breakfast. Chewing aggravated the swelling on his face and only increased the pain, so he had spent the last two days drinking raw milk and sipping on homemade milk shakes. Still, he wondered if some solid food might help him recover from the pounding he took. He stopped in front of the scrambled egg bowl and handed his plate to a short and smiling Hispanic woman behind the counter. The woman smiled even wider as she piled steaming food on his plate.

"Quesadilla?" she said, and gestured to the corn tortillas.

"Oh yes," Jeffrey replied. Already his pain was subsiding.

The woman placed the tortillas on his plate. Impulsively, she reached for a cinnamon roll laced with white cream stripes and added it to his plate. She handed the plate back to Jeffrey with a huge smile.

"Gracias," Jeffrey said.

"Da nada."

They reached the grim-faced cashier at the end of the line. Pablo paid first. When it was Jeffrey's turn, he reached in his pocket and pulled out the wadded up twenty dollar bill that the pockmark-faced Chinese boy had thrown at him. The cashier frowned as Jeffrey unfolded the crinkled bill and handed it to her. She took the bill with her grimy fingers, held it up to the light for inspection, and then rang up his purchase.

Jeffrey picked up his tray and stepped aside. Freshmen students filled in behind him to pay for their food. The cashier reached for her can of diet soda and took a long swig.

Jeffrey and Pablo walked away, carrying their trays. In his best imitation of the cashier's voice, Pablo called over his shoulder, "Move it along back there."

The cashier choked and spit out a long spray of soda.

Freshmen students screamed and jumped out of the way.

Jeffrey sat in the back of the classroom at the end of a long row of desks and stared down at the test paper before him.

The first question read: *You stand in the center of one hundred square miles of wooded terrain. From this position, you travel ten miles east, followed by five miles south, and then two miles directly northwest. From where you now stand, what is the fastest way out of the forest?*

Jeffrey sighed. How the heck did he know? Who came up with these idiot questions? He could hear kids breathing hard all around him. At least he wasn't the only one struggling.

From where you now stand, what is the fastest way out of the forest? Jeffrey wrote *Straight Up*, and went on to the next question.

He glanced at the empty desk to his left and was glad that Marisol Rodriguez wasn't there.

He had known Marisol since the second grade when her family had moved in next door to his. His parents had told him all week that a new family with a girl his age would be moving into the vacant house next door, and Jeffrey had spent that entire Saturday morning peeking out his bedroom window, hoping to catch a glimpse of her. Early in the afternoon, a car with a moving trailer attached, finally pulled into the driveway next door. Lying perfectly still on his bed, Jeffrey watched as the car doors popped open and an eight-year-old girl with knobby knees, light brown skin, and a mass of curly black hair climbed out of the back seat. She was wearing a white T-shirt and red shorts, and Jeffrey watched for over an hour, barely breathing, as the girl helped her mother and her older brother carry boxes from the car to the house. When a knock sounded at his bedroom door, Jeffrey jumped to his feet.

"We're going to say hello to the new neighbors," his mother said. "You want to come?"

Jeffrey stared back at her from behind his glasses, his heart thumping in his throat and shook his head.

His mother eyed him suspiciously. "What are you doing in here?"

"Nothing."

She eyed him a moment longer, and then stepped out of the room, pulling the door closed behind her. Jeffrey spun back to the window, but the girl was gone.

Growing up, he and Marisol shared many of the same classes, but he never dared speak to her. Instead, he spent hours glued to his window, hoping to catch a glimpse of her, and then ducking out of sight on the rare occasions when he did.

It wasn't until the summer before last, when Marisol had asked him and Pablo to help rescue her brother from jail for a crime he didn't commit, that they finally began talking.

Now at age fifteen, they were friends, but little had changed. He still found himself stealing glances at her whenever he could. Watching her as she walked, or brushed her hair back out of her eyes, or gripped a pencil in her fingers – these were the little moments of his day.

He didn't want her to see him like this, with his face bruised and looking like a lump of purple meat. Not that it mattered. He knew she liked Pablo, and he knew that she could never be interested in a fat, clumsy kid in glasses, which is what he was. Still, he could dream.

He heard a rustle at the door and looked up to see Brian McHugh enter the room and approach Mrs. Hammer's desk with a note in his hand. Jeffrey watched as Mrs. Hammer looked up from the book she was reading and took the note. When she finished reading the note, she reached for a test paper, handed it to Brian, and motioned to an empty desk, one aisle over and two seats in front of Jeffrey.

Jeffrey's mouth hung open. Brian McHugh was the last person he wanted to see. Why was he being reassigned to a new class when the semester was almost over? It didn't make sense. It was completely retarded. And why, out of all the classes in their school, was he being reassigned to Jeffrey's?

Brian sauntered down the aisle with a cocky smirk on his face. He slid in behind his desk and immediately squirmed around in his seat to check out his new classmates. When his eyes met Jeffrey's, he burst into laughter. "What happened to you, Jones?"

Mrs. Hammer looked up sharply. Her eyes scanned the class and narrowed when she saw Brian. "Brian, turn around."

Brian spun around in his seat to face Mrs. Hammer, and nodded meekly. He waited for her to resume reading her book, and then turned sideways in his seat and whispered loudly to Jeffrey, "Jones, who messed up your face?"

Jeffrey ignored him. He stared down at the test paper in front of him. Minutes passes as he read the same question over and over, but it was no use. It was impossible to concentrate now.

"Jones," Brian whispered loudly, "what's the answer to number one?"

Jeffrey kept his eyes on his paper.

"Jones!"

Jeffrey kept his head down and made a shooing motion with the back of his hand.

Brian whispered louder. "I need the answer to number one!"

Jeffrey sat back in his seat and hung his head. His face ached, his ribs ached, and he was going to flunk this test. There was no way he was not going to flunk this test. Could life possibly get any worse?

He heard Brian's whispered voice, "Jones, what's the answer to number two?"

Jeffrey took off his glasses and rubbed his eyes. He heard another rustle at the door and put his glasses back on. He looked up and saw Marisol entering the room. She wore the school uniform for girls: a white blouse, a plaid skirt, and dark shoes with white socks.

Marisol handed a note to Mrs. Hammer and spoke to her, gesturing expressively with her arms. Jeffrey couldn't hear what was being said, but it looked like she was apologizing for being late.

Mrs. Hammer handed Marisol a test paper and waved at her to take her seat. Marisol put her hands together and bowed slightly, as if to say thank you, and hurried down the aisle to her desk. She looked at Jeffrey and began to smile, but when she saw his crooked glasses and battered face, her smile vanished.

"Jeffrey, what happened?" she asked in a hoarse whisper as she slid in behind her desk.

"Don't ask."

"Shush!" said Mrs. Hammer.

Jeffrey froze.

Marisol hunched forward and pulled her long black hair down over her face, as if to hide.

Mrs. Hammer lowered her beak-like nose and glowered over the top of her glasses. Her eyes searched the room like prison searchlight beams.

"There's too much talking going on in this classroom. You're supposed to be taking a test, so get on with it. I don't want to hear another word from anyone." She picked up a ruler and slapped it against her desk to emphasize each syllable: "Not-one-more-word."

Heads ducked across the classroom.

Underneath her hair, Marisol scribbled note to Jeffrey: *Did you get in a fight?*

Mrs. Hammer gave the class one more look, then set the ruler down on her desk and picked up her book. The spine of the book read *The Turn of the Screw*.

Marisol lifted her chin. Her brown eyes peaked out from under her maze of hair. Satisfied that no one was watching, she tossed the note on Jeffrey's desk.

Jeffrey read the note from Marisol and scribbled a response: *Wasn't much of a fight. Would've been a lot worse if Pablo wasn't there.* He tossed the note on her desk.

Moments later, her response arrived: *Him too?*

Jeffrey wrote back: *Don't worry. He's okay.*

Mrs. Hammer's ruler landed with a loud swat on her desk. The class jumped. "Thirty more minutes with those tests," she said. A knock sounded at the door. Mrs. Hammer slapped her ruler down on her desk and rose to answer it.

Marisol waited until Mrs. Hammer reached the door, and then tossed another note on Jeffrey's desk: *Are you okay? Are you in pain? Is there anything I can do to help?*

Jeffrey wrote back: *I'm miserable. My life couldn't possibly get any worse.* He slipped the note to Marisol.

"Jeffrey Jones!"

The words from Mrs. Hammer detonated like a bomb in the quiet of the classroom. Jeffrey looked up and saw her staring at him from the classroom door. Standing in the hallway behind her were two men in suits. Mrs. Hammer lifted a bony finger and beckoned Jeffrey forward. "Come here please."

Jeffrey froze like a deer caught in a car's headlights. Desks creaked as bodies twisted in their seats and every face in the room turned his way.

"*Now*, Jeffrey."

Jeffrey felt a knot tighten in his stomach. He rose shakily.

"Be careful, Jeffrey," Marisol whispered.

Jeffrey made the long trek up the aisle towards the front of the room. Every eye in the room followed him. He passed Brian's desk and heard his cackling voice: "Busted!"

The two men standing outside the classroom door studied him carefully, and neither one was smiling. One man was shorter and solidly built; the other was tall and lanky. Behind both men stood the school principal, Mr. Popper, looking nervous and pale-faced, as always.

Jeffrey reached the door. Mrs. Hammer motioned for him to step into the hall with the two men and Mr. Popper. As he did so, she remained in the classroom and closed the door behind her, leaving Jeffrey alone in the hall with the three men. He turned and saw Mrs. Hammer peering at him through the small window in the classroom door. She wagged a frowning finger at his face.

"Jeffrey Jones." The man's voice was a command.

Jeffrey spun around. "Yes?"

"I'm agent White," said the man with the solid build, "and this is agent Stevens." He motioned to the taller man. "Secret Service." Both men flashed their badges. "You're under arrest."

Chapter Nine

"That looks like you," said White.

Jeffrey sat in front of a video monitor in Mr. Popper's office, watching himself on screen as he and Pablo walked down the serving line in the school cafeteria. White stood next to the monitor, holding the remote control in his hand. Stevens stood next to him. Mr. Popper sat in the corner of the room, watching quietly.

"Yes, that's me," Jeffrey said. He watched himself on the monitor as he reached in his pocket and pulled out the wadded up twenty dollar bill that he used to pay for his breakfast.

White nodded at the screen. "And that's you handing over a twenty dollar bill, isn't it?"

"Yes."

White pointed the remote at the screen and froze the video just as Jeffrey passed the bill to the cashier. The agent set the remote control down on Mr. Popper's desk and extracted a pair of latex gloves from his pocket. He slipped the gloves on, reached inside his suit jacket, and removed a clear plastic evidence pouch from the inside pocket. Delicately, he opened the pouch and took out a twenty dollar bill. He held the bill directly in front of Jeffrey's eyes. "Is this the bill you used this morning to pay for your breakfast?"

Jeffrey studied the bill. "I don't know."

"Look at it," Stevens ordered.

"I am."

"Is it the same twenty dollar bill?" asked White.

"It looks the same, but I don't know for sure."

White put the bill back in the clear plastic pouch, and put the pouch back in his pocket. He removed the latex gloves and dropped them in the waste basket.

"It is the same bill," he said. "You gave it to the cashier in the cafeteria this morning. She notified your principal, your principal called the police, and the police called us."

"Why did the police call you?"

"Because that bill is counterfeit."

Jeffrey felt the color drain from his face.

"Do you know what the penalty is for passing counterfeit currency?" Stevens asked.

Jeffrey shook his head.

"Twenty years in prison. Do you want to do twenty years in prison?"

"No sir."

"Then maybe you better tell us."

"Tell you what?"

"Where you're printing those counterfeit bills."

"I didn't print it," Jeffrey protested. "Somebody threw it at me!"

The two men looked at each other.

"It's true," Jeffery insisted. He told them about finding Kevin Wong's body in Mrs. Martin's backyard, the shooting at the hospital, the homicide detectives that questioned both him and Pablo, and the mysterious girl they followed that led to the fight in Monterey Park. "The guy that punched me threw that twenty dollar bill at me. I didn't know it was counterfeit. If I did, I never would have tried using it. I would have called you right away."

"Are you carrying any money on you now?" White asked.

"A little."

"Let's see it."

Jeffrey stood up and emptied his pants pockets on Mr. Popper's desk: house keys, a pen, a comb, fourteen dollars in currency, and fifty-two cents in change. The two men ignored the loose change, but carefully examined the fourteen dollars in currency. Stevens picked up a ten dollar bill and held it up to the light.

"I got that in change this morning," Jeffrey said, "from the cashier in the cafeteria."

White nodded at the breast pocket on Jeffrey's shirt. "What's in there?"

Jeffrey reached in his pocket and pulled out two business cards. He handed them to the agent. White read one of the cards:

THE NORTH HOLLYWOOD DETECTIVE CLUB

Investigation and Deductive Reasoning

Senior Detective: Jeffrey Jones

Senior Detective: Pablo Reyes

White passed a card to Stevens.

Stevens read the card. "Detectives, huh?"

"Yes sir."

Stevens held the business card up and waved it. "Do the police know about this?"

"They know. But they didn't want to hear my theory of the murder."

Both men laughed and Jeffrey felt his face flush hot. Even Mr. Popper laughed, which Jeffrey took as the ultimate insult.

When the laughter died down, White said, "The Los Angeles Police Department has their own way of doing things. Some good, some not so good."

Stevens sighed. "Well, your story corroborates with that of Pablo Reyes."

Jeffrey's eyebrows arched high. "You talked to Pablo?"

The two men looked at each other, but said nothing.

"Third period," said Mr. Popper, from his seat in the corner. All eyes turned his way.

"We talked to Pablo just before you," Stevens said. "He told us the same story."

"Then you knew I was telling the truth," said Jeffrey.

"Not necessarily. But I think it's safe to say that neither of you will be going to jail."

"That's a relief."

White tapped Jeffrey's business card. "Can I keep this?"

Jeffrey nodded.

The agent put Jeffrey's card in his pocket and pulled out one of his own. "You keep this," he said, and handed the card to Jeffrey. "You see any money that looks suspicious, call me."

Jeffrey nodded.

"Just one more thing ..." the agent said.

Jeffrey waited, expectantly.

"I think it's time we called your parents."

"Oh no," Jeffrey said, "anything but that."

Chapter Ten

"How could you do this, Jeffrey?" his mother asked. "How?"

Jeffrey squirmed in the back seat of his father's car. His mother sat twisted around in the front passenger seat, staring directly at him. His father sat behind the wheel, watching him in the rearview mirror.

"Do what?" Jeffrey said.

"Don't give us that 'do what?' nonsense," said his father. He turned the ignition. "You know exactly what we're talking about. You lied to us." He backed the car out of its parking space, and then put the car in drive and accelerated slowly across the school parking lot.

"I didn't lie."

"You *did* lie, Jeffery," said his mother.

"You told us you got those bruises in a fight," said his father.

"I did."

Mr. Jones shot a quick look at Jeffrey in the back seat. "You didn't tell us the fight happened because you were following some girl you don't know. You didn't tell us you were investigating the killing at the hospital."

"You didn't ask."

Mr. Jones stopped the car in the middle of the parking lot. He turned around to face Jeffrey. "What you did was a lie of omission, and you damn well know it. You purposely misled your mother and me."

"I'm sorry," Jeffrey said. "I'm just trying to help people. A guy was murdered and nobody seems to care."

"You don't care about him either."

Mrs. Jones laid her hand on her husband's shoulder. "Brad."

"He doesn't. He talks about helping people, but when he smells a crime he's off like a bloodhound, and he doesn't care who gets hurt or trampled over in the process."

A car horn honked behind them. Mr. Jones ignored it and spoke to his wife. "He wants to solve the murder. He wants to be the big hero, but he doesn't care at all about the poor slob who got shot." He turned back to Jeffrey. "Tell me if I'm wrong, Jeffrey. Tell me if I'm wrong."

Jeffrey sank deeper into the car seat.

As evening fell, his father's anger turned to sarcasm.

"I have to hand it to you, boy," he said. "Getting arrested by the Secret Service, that's a new one."

Jeffrey sat rigidly in his seat at the kitchen table and gazed down at the meatloaf and mashed potatoes growing cold on his plate. "I wasn't arrested."

"No," his father said, "just threatened with arrest. And what was that you did again? What did those agents accuse you of?"

"Passing counterfeit money."

"Passing counterfeit money," his father echoed. He turned to his wife, seated at the table with them. "When Jeffrey was growing up, did you ever imagine that he'd be questioned by the Secret Service for passing counterfeit money?"

Mrs. Jones shook her head slowly. "Never in a million years."

Jeffrey kept his head down.

"By the way," said his father, "how'd you do on that test you were taking when those agents showed up at school?"

"I have to retake it."

"Great, Jeffrey," said his mother.

"You see, son," said his father in a mocking tone, "we just want what's best for you: a good education, a respectable job, perhaps some standing in society. Is that too much to ask?"

Jeffrey didn't respond.

"Your mother and I, we worry about you. We wonder where we went wrong. We wonder what we did in our own lives to deserve a son who finds half-dead bodies lying in the bushes, who gets questioned by the police and the Secret Service, who gets beat up for investigating crimes he has no business investigating, etcetera, etcetera, etcetera."

Jeffrey squirmed.

"Late at night, your mother and I, we talk to each other. We say, 'What should we have done differently? Should we have homeschooled him? Should we have been stricter bringing him up?' To be honest with you, we don't know. Your teachers at school all tell us how smart you are. 'The boy genius,' is the phrase they use. Some of them, anyway. But we don't see the genius, all we see is the trouble: phone calls from the police, phone calls from the Secret Service, phone calls from your school. Perhaps you can tell us, boy genius, just where we went wrong. Perhaps you can tell us just what it is that makes you so insane."

Jeffrey sat in silence.

His mother turned to face him. "Never in my life have I felt so small as I did in front of those Secret Service agents. He asked me if I knew my son was investigating a murder, and I just sat there with my jaw hanging open. He said, 'Don't you know what your son is up to?' I could just feel my face turning bright red. I thought I was going to faint. I just wanted to disappear."

"You didn't answer my question," said his father.

"What question?" Jeffrey asked.

"I said perhaps you can tell us what it is that makes you so insane."

"Is it insane to want to catch a murderer?"

"It's insane for you, at fifteen-years-old, to want to involve yourself in a mess like that."

"I think I can help, Dad."

"I think you can forget it, son."

"But there's a connection between the murder at the hospital and the counterfeit money. I know there is."

"None of your business."

"But Pablo and I are the only ones who saw the killer at the hospital, and we're the only ones who saw the guy who threw that counterfeit twenty dollar bill at me. We're key witnesses to both crimes."

"Not anymore."

"Dad, I could solve this case."

"The only thing you're solving is your homework."

"Why?"

"Because I don't want you getting yourself killed, that's why."

"But it's not fair."

Jeffrey's father slammed the table with his fist. "I don't care whether you think it's fair or not. You're done investigating." He looked at his wife. "He wasn't honest with us because he was afraid we'd take him off the case." He turned back to Jeffrey. "Well, guess what? You're off the case. Understand? Case closed."

Jeffrey pushed back from the table and headed for the basement stairs.

"Jeffrey, sit down," his mother said.

Jeffrey ignored her. He slammed the basement door behind him and clattered down the stairs to his room. Fine, he was off the case. Fine, a man could get shot to death and his killer could escape, free to kill again. If his parents didn't care, if the police didn't care, why should he care? He knew he would feel hungry later for skipping his dinner, but for now he wanted solitude. He wanted time to think and to read.

He went to his bookcase and pulled a pair of books that his grandmother once gave him about the Secret Service. He sank into a beanbag chair next to his bed, cracked open the first book and read late into the night.

Chapter Eleven – 10 Days Before Christmas

Father Pat took one look at Jeffrey's black eye and whistled. "Where'd you get that shiner?"

"Don't ask," Pablo said.

"Uh-oh."

"A couple of guys beat me up," Jeffrey said.

"Sounds like a story you might want to tell me," said Father Pat. He pulled up a stool and lowered himself onto it with a sigh. He and the boys were in the rented basement that Father Pat used to run his private mission. Cartons of canned goods were stacked up high all around them, along with piles of donated clothes. It was here that Jeffrey and Pablo spent their Saturday mornings, helping the retired, white-haired priest they had known since grade school.

"Go ahead, Jeffrey," said Pablo, with a wave of his arm, and Jeffrey related the events of the past few days, from finding Kevin Wong's body up to his talk with the Secret Service.

When Jeffrey finished, Father Pat whistled again. "Counterfeit money, huh? That figures. Seems like the whole world has gone counterfeit."

"What do you mean, Father?" asked Pablo.

"Look at Rome," the priest replied. "We have a counterfeit pope and counterfeit cardinals, leading a counterfeit church and preaching a counterfeit religion. Why, it's been counterfeit for the last fifty years. Rome isn't Catholic anymore, it's pagan. Everything is backwards, everything is upside down." He looked at Jeffrey. "You said these fellows who beat you up were Chinese?"

Jeffrey nodded. "In Monterey Park."

"Sounds like trouble, boys. Sounds like you're messing with the Triads and the Wah Ching."

"The who?" said Pablo.

"Those are Chinese gangs."

"You know about them, Father?"

"Of course, I know. I wasn't born yesterday. Why are you looking so surprised?"

"Because you're a priest."

"So that makes me stupid?"

"No, Father. I didn't mean it like that. I just didn't know that priests knew about gangs and crime and stuff like that."

"You're like everyone else then. You see a white collar and you think I'm some quaint old guy. Listen, I've been a priest since 1962. Do you know how many confessions I've heard?"

Jeffrey and Pablo shook their heads.

"Must be millions by now. I've heard people confess the most vile and disgusting sins imaginable: murder, rape, abortion, crimes against children, and every other kind of sick and immoral behavior. You name it, I've heard it. So why wouldn't I know about the local Chinese gangs?"

"I never thought of it that way," Pablo said. "But it makes perfect sense."

"I never thought of it that way either," said Jeffrey.

"Most people don't," said Father Pat. "They don't realize that there's no one on earth more qualified to comprehend the level of evil, corruption and filth that human beings are capable of stooping to than a traditional Catholic priest."

"Wow," said Pablo.

"Wow," said Father Pat. "Of course, a lot of that misunderstanding comes from the Church itself. Not the true Church, but the counterfeit church that we've had since the Second Vatican Council. It's far worse than this counterfeit money you're talking about. Counterfeit money is a terrible crime, but the counterfeit church that we've had for the last fifty years is leading millions of souls to hell."

The boys sat silently for a long moment. Father Pat had spoken to them many times before about the apostasy taking place in the Church. Both boys and their families had stopped attending the New Mass years ago.

Finally, Jeffrey asked, "What do you know about Chinese gangs, Father?"

"I know plenty, but if you really want some understanding, you should talk to Eddie Lee."

"Who's Eddie Lee?"

"He's a young man of my acquaintance. He was mixed up with these Chinese gangs you're talking about, but he got out. And that's not an easy thing to do. He came to Christ and converted to the true Catholic faith. Today he teaches martial arts. I could call him, if you like, and see if he'd be willing to speak with you."

Jeffrey and Pablo exchanged a quick look.

"Wait here," said Father Pat.

He rose from his stool, paused for a moment to straighten his back, and shuffled his way to a phone in the corner of the basement.

"My dad doesn't want me to do anymore investigating on this case," Pablo whispered.

"Neither does mine," Jeffrey said. "But I guess there's no harm in hearing what this Eddie guy has to say. If he has any information, we can give it to the Secret Service."

"I still have that agent's card," Pablo said.

"Me too," Jeffrey said. "I memorized his phone number."

Father Pat hung up the phone and returned to the boys. "I talked to Eddie. He's waiting for you."

Chapter Twelve

"Do you have a death wish?"

The question caught both Jeffrey and Pablo by surprise.

They exchanged a quick look, before turning back to the young Chinese man, stretching his legs out on the exercise mat before them. Eddie Lee was thirty-years-old, with long black hair pulled back in a ponytail, and dressed in a T-shirt and jeans.

Eddie's dojo was spartan, but functional, and located in a converted garage. A class of aikido students had cleared out moments before and the odor of their sweat lingered with the smell of the straw mats near the entrance, where Jeffrey and Pablo had left their shoes.

The boys stood in their socks on the cold concrete floor, in front of a large, padded exercise mat. Six foot high mirrors lined the walls and above them hung racks of samurai swords. Eddie sat on the mat in a hurdler's stretch. He lowered his forehead to his knee, held it for a few seconds, and then raised his head.

"Why do you ask?" Jeffrey said.

Eddie snorted. "You're asking about the Triads and the Wah Ching, you must have a death wish. He stood up and motioned for Pablo to join him on the mat.

Pablo pointed at himself. "Me?"

"No, the other fifty guys standing over there."

Pablo stepped tentatively onto the mat.

"Hit me," Eddie said.

Pablo hesitated.

"Don't worry," said Eddie. "You're not going to hurt me."

"It's not you I'm worried about."

Eddie laughed. "Come on, I've just insulted your girl. Give me your best punch."

Pablo put up his fists and advanced. Eddie moved with him, his face now set in grim determination. Pablo threw a feint with his left, followed by another. He stepped forward and threw a right cross at Eddie's chin.

Eddie swung his right arm upward in a circle, deflected the punch and slid his right hand down to Pablo's wrist. He placed the palm of his left hand under Pablo's elbow, while simultaneously stepping forward with his left foot and sweeping his right leg back behind him. The next thing Pablo knew his nose was on the mat, with his right arm pinned up behind him. Watching, Jeffrey winced.

Pablo slapped the mat twice with his free hand and Eddie released him.

"Not a bad punch," Eddie said, as Pablo stood up and dusted himself off.

"Yeah, right."

Eddie turned to Jeffrey. "Okay, now it's your turn."

Jeffrey's face paled.

"Jeffrey's not very athletic," Pablo said, hoping to discourage Eddie.

"I can see that. Come on." He motioned for Jeffrey to step onto the mat.

Jeffrey stepped forward tentatively. Eddie grabbed him by the front of his shirt. "Attacker has you like this. What do you do?"

"I don't know," Jeffrey said.

"Extend your arms and spin like a windmill."

Jeffrey did as instructed. He broke Eddie's hold, but spun completely around.

"Never turn you back on your opponent," Eddie said, applying a choke hold on Jeffrey from behind. "Understand?"

Jeffrey nodded and Eddie released him.

"Let's try it again." They faced each other and Eddie grabbed Jeffrey by the shirt with both hands. "Spin sideways, just enough to break the hold."

Jeffrey extended his arms and spun to his right. Eddie leaned his head back as Jeffrey's left hand brushed over his face. The spin broke the hold of Eddie's right hand. "Now follow with a side kick," Eddie said.

"I don't know how."

"Like so." Eddie pivoted on his left foot, brought his right knee up to his chest, and snapped his leg out in a sharp kick. Immediately, he brought his leg back in and lowered his foot to the mat. The entire movement, from pivot to snap took only a second.

Eddie repeated the movement, much slower so Jeffrey could see. "Pivot, raise, and kick."

Jeffrey raised his knee to thigh level, pushed his leg out in a low, wobbly kick, and stumbled across the mat.

"That's the sorriest looking kick I've ever seen," Eddie said. "All right, try this."

He reached in his pocket, pulled out a switchblade knife and flicked the blade open.

"Whoa," said Pablo.

"Don't worry, it's fake. It's a movie prop. See?" He slid his fingers over the plastic blade. He handed the knife to Jeffrey. "Stick me."

"How?"

"Any way you can."

Jeffrey balanced the prop knife in his hand and thrust it out tentatively.

Eddie danced back. His eyes narrowed into slits and his jaw hardened. "Come on, we're even now. You got the knife."

Pablo watched as Jeffrey lunged forward with the knife. Eddie danced back. Jeffrey switched to an overhand grip. Eddie stepped closer. Jeffrey raised the knife, rushed forward, and brought his hand down in a stabbing motion.

Eddie sidestepped the blade, grabbed Jeffrey by the wrist and swung his arm down and then all the way back in a circle. Jeffrey's body followed his arm, his feet left the mat, and he flew head over heels and landed on his back with a thump on the mat.

"Whoa!" said Pablo. "Are you okay, Jeffrey?"

Jeffrey blinked up at the dojo ceiling. "I think so."

"He's fine," said Eddie. He extended his hand and helped pull Jeffrey to his feet.

"How did you do that?" Pablo gushed. "It looked like something in a movie. And how come Jeffrey's not hurt?"

"Because I didn't intend for him to get hurt. There are two kinds of aikido. In the first form of aikido, it is assumed that whoever chooses to fight has broken his connection to the universe. It is up to the aikido practitioner to restore that connection by using as little force as possible. In that way, aikido is a healing art."

"What's the second kind of aikido?" Pablo asked.

"Combat aikido. In that case, aikido is as deadly a martial art as any. Some say the deadliest." He took the prop knife back from Jeffrey. "What do you do if someone comes at you with a real knife or with one of those swords on the wall?" He motioned to the samurai swords above the mirrors.

"We die?" Jeffrey said.

"No, you run. There's no shame in running when your attacker is armed and you're not. Remember, he who runs away today, lives to fight another day." He returned the prop knife to his pocket. "On the other hand, you can always improvise a weapon."

He removed his black leather belt and snapped it taut between his hands. "See? Or like this." He wrapped the belt around his right hand, leaving twelve inches of slack with the buckle at the end. "That belt buckle can cut an ugly gash. When your life's at stake, you take what your surroundings give you."

"Did you learn aikido in China?" Pablo asked.

"No, aikido is a Japanese art. To beat the Wah Ching, I had to think differently. So I learned something they weren't expecting. It wasn't easy. They gave me this to remember them by." He lifted his shirt to reveal an eight inch jagged scar stitched across his abdomen. The boys winced.

"Maybe now you'll tell me why you want to know about them."

"We're investigating a case," Jeffrey said.

"We *were* investigating," Pablo put in. "We're not anymore."

Jeffrey shrugged sheepishly. "Our parents don't want us investigating. They told us to drop the case."

"What kind of case?"

"Murder."

Eddie nodded. "Well, your parents have good reason to be alarmed."

Jeffrey handed Eddie a business card. Eddie read the card and snapped his fingers. "Wait a second, I've heard about you. Aren't you the guys who found that treasure, and helped that guy get out of jail?"

Jeffrey nodded. "That was us."

"And now you're mixed up with Chinese gangs. Well, you might be in over your heads on this one."

"What can you tell us about the Chinese gangs?" Jeffrey asked.

"In a word: deadly." Eddie waved the boys over to a wooden bench by the dojo's entrance. They all sat down.

"The Chinese gangs aren't showy like the Bloods, or the Crips, or the Mexican gangs. But don't let that fool you. In an all-out street war, the Chinese gangs would wipe the floor with the other gangs. If you want to understand Los Angeles street gangs, you have to start with the mentality of the average gangster. People who gravitate to street gangs are ignorant hoods. I know, I used to be one myself."

Eddie paused for a moment and then continued. "With most gangs, it's an image thing. They think drugs and street crime are cool, and it's the only way they get props from their peers, who are other ignorant hoods. If someone gets hurt or killed in the process, they don't care. The drugs and the street culture have corrupted their minds to the point that they're incapable of feeling sympathy for any of their victims. In a sense, they've lost the ability to think. The Chinese gangs are different."

Eddie tapped the side of his forehead. "The Asian mind is very cunning, and smarter than most. And most Asian gangsters couldn't care less about projecting an image. You could pass a Chinese gangster on the street and never even know it. Sure, they have their share of ignorant hoods on the street level; the ones out carjacking and doing home invasions. But beyond that, the Chinese gangs are quite sophisticated. They prefer white collar crime: insurance fraud, bank fraud, counterfeiting."

"Counterfeiting?" Jeffrey said, and he Pablo both sat up.

"Yeah. You know something I don't?"

Jeffrey told Eddie about their encounter with the Chinese boys and the counterfeit twenty dollar bill. Eddie nodded. "It takes brains and planning to produce counterfeit currency. The other gangs can't do it, but the Asian gangs can. It's odd though, because that bill you passed must not have been very good if your school cashier knew it was phony." He motioned at Jeffrey. "You say the guy who punched you had pockmarks on his face?"

"Yeah, and he had a crooked nose, like it was broken before."

"And the Chinese girl you were following?"

"She was hot," Pablo said. The others turned to him and he blushed. "I mean, you know, for someone involved in a murder."

"I get the idea," Eddie said.

"She was around fifteen-years-old," Jeffrey said. "Straight black hair, parted in the middle. And pretty, like Pablo said. She looked like a model."

"Let me poke around," Eddie said. "I'll see what I can find." He held up the business card that Jeffrey gave him. "I can call you at this number?"

Jeffrey nodded.

"Okay," Eddie said. "I'll see what I can do."

"We appreciate your help," Jeffrey said, "but if these gangs are as deadly as you say, maybe you'd better not."

Eddie laughed. "Don't worry about me. I've handled the Triads and the Wah Ching before. There's just one thing."

The boys looked at him, expectantly.

"Don't mention my name to anyone you talk to," Eddie said, "especially the police. I don't want them snooping around here asking questions."

Chapter Thirteen - 8 Days Before Christmas

Jeffrey sat hunched over a book in a corner of the school library, reading about the Secret Service. It was his lunch period, but neither Pablo nor Marisol shared the same schedule, and Jeffrey was ashamed to be seen eating his lunch alone in the school cafeteria, so he spent his lunch periods in the library and made friends with books. By the time he got home, he was famished, but he wondered if skipping lunch might help him lose weight.

The thick volume he was reading now was much more detailed about the Secret Service than the books his grandmother had given him. He knew that the Secret Service was tasked with protecting the President and the Vice-President and their families, but he didn't know that the agency was actually created in 1865 to combat a wave of counterfeit currency that appeared after the Civil War. It wasn't until 1901, when President William McKinley was assassinated, that the Secret Service began protecting presidents and presidential candidates.

A shadow fell over the page he was reading and he looked up to see Susie Norris standing beside his table. She took one look at Jeffrey and shrieked, "What happened to your face?"

Kids seated at tables around them admonished her to hush.

Miss Hornsby, the spinsterish school librarian, heard the commotion and looked up from the book she was reading. Tufts of gray hair stood out furiously from the side of her head. She straightened her glasses and peered across the library from her perch behind the checkout counter.

Susie slid into a seat across the table from Jeffrey and lowered her voice to a whisper. "What happened to your face?"

Jeffrey squirmed uncomfortably and whispered back, "Nothing."

"You look like you were hit by a truck. Does it hurt?"

"Only when I breathe."

"Very funny. Well, you just ruined my plans."

Jeffrey eyed her suspiciously. "What plans?"

Susie placed a finger on the center of her glasses and pushed them up to the top of her nose. "I'm the volunteer activities director at the children's orphanage and I was going to ask you to play Santa Claus at our Christmas party tomorrow."

Jeffrey stared back at her, his face like stone. "Santa Claus?"

"Sure, you'd be perfect. You're round, you're jolly – sometimes, anyway – and you could totally do it without any padding."

Jeffrey felt a burn rising in his cheeks. "Thank you for that intelligent observation."

"I'm just sayin'."

Jeffrey ignored her and resumed reading.

Susie sat back in her chair. "Well forget it now. I can't have a Santa Claus with a black eye."

"Ho, ho, ho."

"You see," Susie said, leaning forward in her seat. "You'd be perfect. Oh, Jeffrey." She rested her chin in her hands and watched him as he read. His bulk spilled out of his chair and over the table and his lips moved almost imperceptibly to the words he was reading. Susie frowned. "Why do you have to be so big? It's not good for your heart, you know."

"Since when do you care about my heart?"

"I don't, but Marisol and Pablo are my friends, and I know if anything happened to you, they would be crushed. So for their sakes, you need to lose weight."

Jeffrey looked up from his book and fixed her with a withering stare.

"Don't look at me like that," Susie said. "What if there was a fire in here, and you had to run for your life? Did you ever think about that? You wouldn't make it. I'd be out of here like a shot, but you ... you'd be a crispy critter."

Jeffrey shook his head and went back to his book. Susie glanced around the room, populated with pale, pinch-faced students, hunched over their textbooks, tablets and smart phones. The library's heater was on and the room lacked ventilation, which magnified its musty smell. "What are you doing in here anyway?" she whispered to Jeffrey. "You need fresh air. You need a life."

Jeffrey kept his eyes glued to his book. "I have a life. And right now that life is performing an activity you may have heard of before. It's called reading. You should try it sometime."

"Ha-ha."

"My brain is expanding."

"So is your waistline."

Jeffrey slammed his book closed. In the quiet of the library, it sounded like a trench mortar. Heads snapped from every direction.

He whispered harshly. "Don't you have anything better to do?"

"Don't *you* have anything better to do?" She glanced down at his book. "What are you reading anyway?"

"Nothing," Jeffrey said, placing his arm over the book's cover.

Susie leaned her head sideways, flat on the table, and read the book's spine. "Secret Service? Why are you reading about the Secret Service? Are you working on a new case?"

"No."

"Yes, you are. I can smell it. Who are you investigating?"

Jeffrey's voice rose with anger. "I'm not investigating anyone!"

Across the library, books and smart phones lowered. Inquisitive eyes turned their way.

Miss Hornsby sat up stiff and straight in her chair and scanned the library.

Susie hunched low over the table. "You lie," she whispered. "Never mind. I'll ask Pablo. He'll tell me."

"No, he won't."

"Yes, he will. Pablo appreciates my female charm. That's something you don't understand."

Jeffrey rose out of his chair and his voice rose with him. "Is this how you spend your time?"

Scattered voices shushed him.

Jeffrey slid back into his seat and lowered his voice. "Is this how you spend your time? Dreaming up ways to antagonize me?"

"Don't flatter yourself, buster. I've got more important things to do than to spend my time antagonizing you."

"Then go do them."

"Fine. Be that way. I don't have to sit here and take your insults. I'm just trying to help."

"You're not trying to help at all. You came in here hoping to con me into playing Santa Claus for a bunch of orphan kids. Let me tell you something, I wouldn't play Santa Claus for all the tea in China."

Susie sat straight up in her chair. "Boy, was I wrong. You're not Santa Claus, you're Scrooge."

"That's better than being a – a nosy old hag!"

Susie gasped and covered her mouth. Heads turned from across the room.

"Jeffrey Jones!" Miss Hornsby spoke with an arch pitch. She was standing behind the checkout counter, her eyes peering at Jeffrey from behind her spectacles.

Jeffrey turned around in his seat and faced her.

Miss Hornsby drew herself up. "How dare you, young man? Simply how dare you! Why, it's bad enough that you raise your voice in the *library*," she drew out the word in the most haughty way. "But to raise your voice to such a sweet young girl ... Why, I don't know what!"

Jeffrey rose out of his chair. "Sweet young girl?" He pointed across his chest at Susie. "You mean *her?*"

The library exploded in laughter.

Miss Hornsby rocked back on her heels, aghast.

Susie buried her face in her hands.

Chapter Fourteen

Footsteps tapped across the patio outside Jeffrey's kitchen door. A key turned in the lock. The door creaked open and Jeffrey stepped inside, followed by Pablo.

"I was so mad, I could have killed her," Jeffrey said.

"I'd be mad too if she got me in trouble."

Jeffrey used the heel of his foot to swing the door shut. "The last day of school before Christmas break and I had to stay an hour late emptying trash. I must have emptied every waste basket in the school, and that was *after* I apologized to her. And the worst part of it was I didn't do anything. All I wanted was for her to leave me alone."

They took off their jackets and draped them over the back of two chairs at the kitchen table.

Pablo eyed a pull-up bar mounted above the door frame leading to the living room and stepped closer to it. "Is that new?"

"It's my dad's."

"You should use it."

"I'd pull the whole wall down."

Pablo took hold of the bar with an underhand grip and began knocking out chin-ups in perfect form.

Jeffrey opened a squeaking cabinet door and pulled out two clean glasses. He set them on the table.

Pablo finished his set. His feet touched down on the floor. He spread his arms wide, and then pulled them across his chest, stretching and flexing.

Jeffrey opened the refrigerator door and removed a gallon of raw milk. "This is the stuff I was telling you about. It's one hundred percent raw from grass-fed cows. We can get it here in California."

He filled both glasses with milk.

Pablo reached for a glass and took a sip. "This is great."

"Isn't it?" Jeffrey reached for the other glass and downed it in a series of long swallows. "This is just too good." He refilled his glass. "Oh, and get this: I have to go down to that orphanage where she works tomorrow afternoon and help out for two hours."

"Oh, man. Those poor kids."

"Forget the kids. Poor me." He took another swill of milk.

"Maybe your dad's right," Pablo said.

"About what?"

"You're a lightning rod for trouble."

"Thanks a lot."

The kitchen phone rang. Jeffrey set his glass on the table and checked the caller ID.

"It's Eddie Lee," he said excitedly. He reached for the receiver. "Hello?"

"Jeffrey Jones?" the voice on the line asked.

"Yes, it's me."

"Eddie Lee here. Listen, I've been poking around. I have some information for you."

Jeffrey turned to Pablo and made a scribbling motion with his hands. Pablo's eyes darted about the room. He spotted a notepad and a pen on the kitchen counter, grabbed them, and handed them to Jeffrey.

"Yes, Mr. Lee," Jeffrey said. "I'm all ears."

Eddie sat at a desk in his office at the dojo. Behind him, a window faced the brick wall of an alley. "I'm still looking for the girl you told me about, the one who looks like a model, but the guy that roughed you up – the one with the pockmarked face – his name is Thomas Chan. He's a punk, a gang member. Been arrested a dozen times. He's one of those ignorant hoods I told you about."

Jeffrey cradled the phone between his shoulder and his ear, and wrote the name down. "What else can you tell me about him?"

Eddie leaned back in his chair and twirled the phone cord in his fingers. "He's been busted for vandalism, assault, petty theft; just an ignorant hood. I actually knew his father back in the day. He was good with a knife, but a strange looking dude. He only had one eye. The story is he took on five guys in a knife fight. He got three of them, but the other two sliced him up pretty bad and left him out in the desert to die. The vultures thought he actually *was* dead and gouged out one of his eyes. I remember his one good eye had this strange yellow tint. He was a hood, too. Like father, like son, I guess. At least the old man had some brains. The son, Thomas, is dumb as a rock. I got an address." He told Jeffrey the address and Jeffrey wrote it down.

"This is good information," Jeffrey said. "Thanks for passing it on."

"There's something else."

Jeffrey gripped the phone tightly. "I'm listening."

Eddie furrowed his brow. "Well, I can't quite put my finger on it, but word on the street is something big is about to happen. Could be a gang war, could be something else, I don't know. Whatever it is, nobody's talking. And I mean *nobody*. If I find out anything more, I'll let you know."

"Thank you, Mr. Lee."

"Stay out of trouble." Eddie said, and hung up the phone.

Jeffrey hung up the phone in the kitchen and leaned back against the counter. He handed the notepad to Pablo.

"Thomas Chan," Pablo said, reading the name off the pad.

"That's Pockmark Face," Jeffrey said. "He's a smalltime hood."

Pablo held up the pad. "We should take this to the police."

Jeffrey shook his head. "I'm not so sure." He told Pablo what Eddie reported to him just before he hung up.

Pablo whistled. "It's just like you said, Jeffrey: a crime bigger than murder."

"Only we don't know what the crime is."

"All the more reason to go to the police," Pablo said.

"Do you think they would believe us?"

"Probably not, but still we should try. At the very least, they could arrest this Thomas Chan for assault."

Jeffrey nodded. "You're probably right. But here's the thing: If whatever is going to happen is serious enough that they would make two attempts to kill someone – first by shooting Kevin Wong and dumping his body in Mrs. Martin's yard, and then again at the hospital when they realized they hadn't finished the job – then they won't hesitate to kill again. And now that Eddie Lee is involved, well, I don't want to put him in any danger."

"Wouldn't it be less dangerous for Eddie if we told the police?"

"Tell them what? All we really have is that name. I guess I could press charges for assault. But if we tell them we heard that some kind of massive crime might be happening, they'd ask us what the crime was and how we knew, and then we'd have to give them Eddie's name."

"And he told us not to do that."

"Right. Even if we give them Thomas Chan's name, they're going to ask where we got it." Jeffrey frowned. "I should have told Eddie to be careful before I hung up."

"A guy like that? He can take care of himself." Pablo handed the notepad back to Jeffrey. "I still think you should give that name to the police, though. Throw that punk in jail. You can tell them you found his name on your own."

"Let me think about it for a day or two. Maybe we can find out more if Thomas Chan isn't in jail."

Pablo raised an eyebrow. "Does that mean we're back on the case?"

Jeffrey sighed. "I don't know, Pablo. My dad told me to drop it, but that was before we had this latest news. If there's some huge crime about to take place, and we could have stopped it, but we don't, I'll never forgive myself. We have to ask ourselves: is it okay to commit a small sin in order to possibly prevent a larger sin from taking place?"

Pablo frowned. He didn't know the answer.

Back at the dojo, Eddie sat for a long time at his desk. Finally, he rose and stepped out of his office. Outside the window behind his desk, a shadow passed by the alley.

Chapter Fifteen – 7 Days Before Christmas

Jeffrey stared back at Susie with a look of utter disbelief. "If you think I'm putting that costume on, you're crazy."

"It's not a costume," Susie said, "it's a Santa Claus suit." She held the red wool suit, the red cap with the white furry ball at the end, and the fluffy white beard up at eye level for Jeffrey to see.

"What's the difference?"

Susie lowered her arms. She and Jeffrey faced each other in a small office at the orphanage where she worked. "Costumes are for super heroes. This," she raised the red suit back up to eye level, "is for *Santa Claus*. I promised the children that Santa Claus was coming to visit today."

"Well, it looks like you're going to have to break your promise."

"You can't be serious."

"I am serious, and stop trying to make me feel guilty."

"You should feel guilty. Anyone who would treat children as cruelly as you deserves to be racked with guilt." She dropped the red suit on a desk in the center of the room.

"I'm not being cruel. I'm being truthful."

"You're being cruel."

"I'm not going to lie to a bunch of kids."

"It's not lying."

"It *is* lying. You're telling them that some made up character is a real person. Then they find out later that it's not true and they end up hating you for the rest of their life."

"No, they don't."

Jeffrey raised a finger. "I distinctly remember when I was nine-years-old and I found out that Santa Claus wasn't real. I was sitting in my third grade class, writing a letter to the North Pole when Brian McHugh saw what I was doing, laughed in my face, and told me Santa Claus wasn't real. I'll never forget it. I was so mad at my parents for lying to me all those years that I didn't talk to either one of them for over a week."

"Now you're being overly dramatic."

"I'm not being overly dramatic. I'm telling you how kids feel. It's even worse with orphan kids like you have here. They don't have parents to get mad at, so they're going to get mad at you. And they're never going to trust you or anyone else ever again."

Susie waved her arm dismissively. "Well, it didn't bother me when I found out Santa wasn't real. I love my Christmas memories. When I was growing up, believing in Santa Claus was wonderful. It's part of the magic of childhood."

"Magic of childhood? There's no magic of childhood. When I was a kid I got beat up and yelled at all the time."

"I can see why."

Jeffrey's face flamed red. "Why do you have to lie to these kids? Why can't you just tell them the truth?"

"What's the truth?"

"Life is horrible and then you die."

"Oh, please, Jeffrey."

"Christmas isn't about Santa Claus," Jeffrey insisted, "it's about the birth of Jesus."

"I know that, and we can talk to the children about that, but just this one little time can't we play pretend? I want to see their little faces light up when they see Santa Claus."

"Won't their faces light up when they see me?"

"Hardly. They don't want to see *you*. They want to see Santa Claus."

"What am I, chopped liver?"

"You're not Santa Claus."

"Well, I'm not doing it."

"Please, Jeffrey?"

"No, I said no. I'll be happy to talk to those kids about Jesus and the meaning of Christmas, but I'm not going to lie to them about Santa Claus."

"But these are little children."

"Stop with the little children."

"But they *are* little children."

"Too bad."

"Well, bah-humbug to you too." Susie plopped down in the chair behind her desk. "Don't you know Santa Claus was a saint? Old Saint Nick?" She shook her head. "Poor orphan children and you're going to ruin their Christmas."

"Don't put this on me," Jeffrey said. "I told you at the library I don't like Santa Claus, I don't believe children should be lied to about Santa Claus, and I'm not going to dress up like Santa Claus."

"Yeah, yeah, yeah." Susie swiveled her chair so she faced the window with her back to Jeffrey. She gazed out at the parking lot outside.

"If you want to give those kids Santa Claus so bad," Jeffrey said, "why don't you wear the costume?"

"I'm sure that would go over big."

"I'm sure it would. You could have hired someone."

Susie spun around in her chair to face him. "We're on a budget here, Jeffrey. I thought that maybe – just maybe – you would do me this one teeny little favor as a friend. I guess I was wrong. I didn't realize you were so selfish."

"*Selfish!*"

"That's what you are. Always thinking of yourself."

"I'm getting pretty tired of people calling me selfish."

Susie sighed and rose out of her chair. "Well, come on. If you're going to break their little hearts, we might as well get it over with." She stepped to the door, reached for the doorknob and stopped. "Please, Jeffrey? One last chance?"

Jeffrey folded his arms firmly over his chest and shook his head. "I'm not dressing up like Santa Claus, I'm not dressing up like Santa Claus, I'm not dressing up like Santa Claus. And that's final."

Susie scowled and opened the door. She stepped into the adjoining room. Jeffrey followed her.

A dozen children, aged four and five, filled the room. A brown-haired little boy played with blocks on the carpeted floor. A blond-haired little girl spun a huge globe mounted on a stand. A red-headed little girl pulled leather-bound books from one of the shelves that covered the four walls of the room and let them fall to the floor. They all turned as Susie stepped into the room and announced, "Hello, everyone. I brought a friend to play with us today."

The children observed Susie and Jeffrey silently.

A chubby little girl with curly brown hair stepped closer and pointed at Jeffrey's stomach. "You're fat."

"And you're a midget," Jeffrey said.

Susie smacked his arm.

"Ow!" Jeffrey winced and rubbed his arm.

"Ha-ha," said the little girl.

"Ha-ha yourself," said Jeffrey.

"Where's Santa Claus?" a little boy asked.

"Santa couldn't make it today," Susie said.

A dozen stoic little faces stared back at Susie for a moment, and then suddenly burst into tears.

Susie folded her arms over her chest and looked at Jeffrey sideways. Her eyes said, "I told you so."

Jeffrey's eyes said something else. He stormed back to the office and slammed the door. The shrieking children turned to Susie.

Jeffrey could feel the blood in his veins pumping furiously. He paced from one end of the office to the other, his face and neck as red as the Santa Claus suit that lay crumpled on the desk. From the other room came the moaning sobs of the children and Susie's voice, urging them to shush.

Jeffrey turned to the window and the parking lot outside. For a brief moment, he thought of opening the window, climbing out and running all the way home. The cries of the children grew louder and echoed off the office walls. "I knew she was going to do this," he muttered to himself. "I knew it."

He tugged off his jacket and dropped it over the back of the desk chair. Then he took off his glasses, placed them on the desk, and reached for the white beard and the red suit.

Five minutes later, the office door flew open and Santa Claus greeted the children in a deep baritone voice. "Ho! Ho! Ho!"

The children turned to the red-suited figure and screamed. Like a swarm of bees, they rushed to him, tugging on his legs and leaping for joy.

"Ho! Ho! Ho!" Jeffrey said again. Without his glasses everything was a blur.

The chubby little girl pulled on his pants leg, while another child yanked on his sleeve. Jeffrey stumbled sideways, struggling to keep his balance.

Susie rushed to his aid and steadied him. "Easy now," she told the children. "Don't make Santa dizzy."

She took Jeffrey by the arm and guided him to an armchair near the fireplace. Jeffrey plopped down on the seat and the children swarmed around him.

Susie's cell phone rang. She fished the phone out of her pocket and answered it.

"Have you all been good?" Jeffrey asked the children in his baritone voice.

The children nodded and a chorus of voices said, "Yes."

"I have to take this call," Susie announced.

Jeffrey turned to her with a look of panic. Susie saw the desperation in his eyes and whispered, "Don't be a baby." To the children, she said, "I'll be right back. Be nice to Santa." She lifted the phone to her ear, said "Hello," and walked out of the room. Jeffrey's hands began to tremble.

"What happened to your eye, Santa?" asked the brown-haired boy.

"Oh, just a little accident. Those reindeer are feisty, you know."

"Santa, where are your presents?" a child asked.

"What did you bring us?" said another.

The chubby little girl hoisted herself up on the wooden arm of the chair and patted Santa's stomach. "You're fat," she said.

"Ho! Ho! Ho! Santa is supposed to be fat."

The girl grinned and patted her own stomach. "I'm fat too."

More children clamored for presents.

"My presents are all at the North Pole," Jeffrey said.

"Why didn't you bring them?" asked the red-headed girl.

"Because I have something better than presents. I have a game to play."

"What's the game?" asked the blond-haired girl.

"The game is called Jeffrey's Kingdom."

"Who's Jeffrey?"

"Jeffrey's the king, and right now he's up in his castle, reading books and eating chocolate ice cream."

Envious faces stared back at him. A wide-eyed little boy licked his lips.

Jeffrey continued: "King Jeffrey needs a court." He pointed to the brown-haired little boy. "You will be the commander of the royal army. Your job is to build a castle of blocks to protect the kingdom from invaders."

The boy swelled with pride.

Jeffrey's eyes searched the children. He pointed to a bug-eyed little boy with puffy hair that bulged out on either side of his head. "And you will be the court jester. Your job is to make the king laugh."

The boy stared back at him with a blank look. Jeffrey waved his arm over the other children. "The rest of you are all peasants."

"What's a peasant?" asked the blond-haired girl.

"A peasant tills the land," Jeffrey said, "and builds the roads and bridges, and provides food and comfort to everyone in the kingdom."

"I don't want to be a peasant," the chubby girl said. "I want to be a princess."

"Ho! Ho! Ho! There are no princesses in Jeffrey's kingdom, only Jeffrey the king."

"Then I don't want to play."

"But you have to play."

"No, I don't."

"Don't you know," Jeffrey began, speaking in his normal voice. He caught himself and switched back to his deep baritone, "Don't you know that being a peasant in Jeffrey's kingdom is better than being a princess in any other kingdom in the world?"

The girl stared back at him.

"Well, it's true," Jeffrey said. "Everyone wants to be a peasant in Jeffrey's kingdom. Now does everyone want to play?"

"Yes," answered a chorus of voices.

Minutes later, Susie returned to the room. Jeffrey was still in his chair with the children seated on the floor in front of him. The chubby little girl turned and looked up at Susie, eyes shining. "Look, Susie, I'm a peasant."

Susie stopped and rocked back on her heels. "A what?"

"A peasant."

"I'm a peasant too," said a little boy.

"We're all peasants," said a second little boy. "Except for Jeffrey, he's the king."

Susie flashed a fake smile. "Oh, really?"

Jeffrey shrugged sheepishly. In his Santa Claus voice, he said, "Such a fun game we're playing."

"Will you play with us, Susie?" asked the chubby girl.

Susie kept the fake smile plastered on her face. "Not right now, honey." She put her hands on her hips. "Can I see you for a second, Santa? Alone."

"Ho! Ho! Ho!" Jeffrey said. "That lady wants to see me." He pushed himself out of the chair.

A chorus of protesting young voices chimed in.

"Don't worry, children," Jeffrey told them. "I'm going to remember all of you on Christmas morning."

Susie opened the office door and motioned for Jeffrey to step inside. He waved at the children and stepped into the office. The children waved back and shouted, "Bye, Santa!" Susie followed Jeffrey into the office. She turned in the doorway to smile and wave at the children. In a sing-song voice, she told them, "I'll be right back." Then the door narrowed and closed.

Inside the small office, Jeffrey said, "You can wipe that silly grin off your face."

Susie turned to him with a look of fury. "What do you think you're doing?"

Jeffrey shrugged. "I was playing with the kids."

"You call that playing? Calling them all peasants?"

"It's just a game."

"It's not a game, it's disgusting. And you – Oh!" She clenched both fists and shook them.

"Calm down."

"Don't tell me to calm down. I'm so angry with you right now I could scream."

"Angry about what?"

"About *you!*"

"Now wait a second," Jeffrey said, getting mad himself. "I didn't want to do this to begin with, but you conned me into it."

"Nobody conned you into anything."

"Yes, you did. *'Oh, the poor children! Oh! Oh!'* That's not a con?" He tore the Santa Claus cap off his head and threw it on the desk. "You made me feel so guilty, I had no choice."

"That's your excuse for exploiting children?"

"I didn't exploit anyone." Jeffrey ripped the big white beard off his face and threw it on the desk. "They were having fun. They enjoyed being peasants."

Susie threw up her hands.

"I'm serious," Jeffrey said. "If you had taken five minutes to observe before passing judgment, you'd have seen that we were all having fun."

"I'm sure you were."

"Not just me, all of us. In fact, you should have joined us. You'd make a perfect peasant."

Susie pointed at the door. "Out. Out of this building."

Jeffrey started for the door.

"Not that way," Susie shrieked in his ear. "The children will see you."

Jeffrey unbuttoned the red shirt of his costume and removed it. Underneath, he was wearing the jeans and T-shirt he came in. "From now on, the answer is no." He flung the red top across the room and reached for the fat square buckle on his belt. "The next time you want me to participate in one of your little schemes, the answer is no."

Susie folded her arms over her chest. "Don't worry; there won't be a next time."

"That suits me just fine." Jeffrey unbuckled the black belt and unzipped the red pants. "I'm not a trained seal." He yanked the red pants down to his knees. "I don't exist in life for your personal amusement." He lifted his foot to step out of the pants. "And I'm not as stupid as you think." His foot caught on the clothing and he pitched forward, hitting the floor with an ugly splat.

A knock sounded at the door.

"Yes?" Susie called.

A child's voice asked, "Where's Santa Claus?"

"We're coming," Susie said. "Just one minute."

Jeffrey rolled onto his back on the floor. He kicked his legs furiously, trying to free himself of the red costume pants. Susie took hold of one of the pant legs and pulled as Jeffrey kicked. The red pants pulled free and Susie fell back against the wall, holding the red pants in her hand. Jeffrey stood up, panting. His face was beet red.

"I can't leave the children alone," Susie said. "Wait until I've cleared the room and then you can leave. I don't want them putting two and two together and figuring out you were Santa Claus."

"Forget it," Jeffrey said, "I'll use the window." He snatched his glasses off the desk where he'd left them and put on his jacket.

Another knock sounded at the door.

"I'm coming," Susie called.

Jeffrey flipped the latch on the office window. It swung open with a squeaking hinge. A cold December wind filled the room.

Susie watched as he lifted a leg to climb out. "Jeffrey, wait," she said, a tinge of remorse in her voice.

He ignored her and climbed out onto a gravel bed that crunched under his shoes. He stepped across the gravel to the asphalt parking lot. Behind him, he heard the squeaking hinge of the window and the sound of it snapping closed.

He stalked his way across the parking lot, punching his thigh with the bottom of his fist and scolding himself for being so stupid. Never again would he allow himself to be taken advantage of like that. Never again would he humiliate himself by wearing such a stupid costume.

Halfway across the parking lot, he suddenly stopped. The costume ...? Of course!

As much as he hated Susie Norris, she'd just given him a scathingly brilliant idea.

Chapter Sixteen – 6 Days Before Christmas

Marisol roared with laughter. "Jeffrey, is that you?"

Jeffrey stood before her in his living room, dressed all in black with a black beret atop his head, black clip-on shades over his glasses, and a pencil-thin black mustache pasted over his upper lip.

He removed his black beret with a flourish and bowed deeply at the waist. "Oui, mademoiselle," he said, with a French accent. "May I escort you to zee Eiffel Tower?"

Marisol rolled back on the couch, laughing uncontrollably and punching the cushions.

Jeffrey extended his arm towards the hallway. "And may I introduce Master Reyes."

Marisol looked past him to the hall, but saw nothing.

"Master Reyes," Jeffrey called to the empty hallway, "zee young lady awaits you."

Marisol looked again. Still nothing.

Jeffrey inserted his pinky fingers into the corners of his mouth and whistled loudly.

The door to the hallway bathroom opened and Pablo stepped out. He strode into the living room, dressed in blue jeans and a blue turtleneck shirt, with a blue beret perched rakishly atop his head. A blue scarf hung loosely around his neck. Pablo took one end of the scarf and threw it dramatically over his shoulder. "Haw, haw, haw! Zee princess is here!"

Marisol screamed with laughter. She rolled over on the sofa cushions and stamped the floor with her feet.

The boys watched her, grinning.

"It's not *that* funny," Pablo said.

"Yes, it is!" Marisol said, gripping her side to ease the pain of laughing so hard. When she had recovered enough to speak, she shouted, "You guys are crazy."

"Oui," Jeffrey said in his French accent. "We may be crazy, but we are very clever." In his normal voice, he added, "What do you think of our disguises?"

Marisol fanned her face with her hand and looked them over. "Pablo, is that really you?"

"Oui, madam. It is I."

"Will you take me to the Eiffel Tower?"

Pablo bowed. "I shall escort you to zee ends of zee Earth. First stop, zee City of Lights."

Marisol smiled and clapped her hands.

"Actually," Jeffrey said, "Paris isn't the City of Lights anymore. It's turned into a dump."

Pablo removed his beret and spoke in his normal voice. "Not just Paris, but all of France."

"All of France," Jeffrey repeated.

"I still want to go," Marisol said.

"No, you don't," Pablo told her. "Paris, London, Sweden, they're all dumps now. There's trash everywhere, and crime. People get stabbed just walking down the street. You don't want to go there."

"They're nice places to get stabbed," Jeffrey said, "but I wouldn't want to live there."

Marisol shook her head. "You guys are crazy. Why are you wearing those disguises?"

The boys exchanged a look.

Marisol noticed and sat up straight. "Are you working on a new case?"

Jeffrey nodded. "We were going to ask you to join us on a little scouting expedition, only it's a little dangerous."

"Don't worry about me," Marisol said. "Danger is my middle name."

"Hey, that's my line," Pablo said.

"Great minds think alike, don't they, Jeffrey?" Marisol looked from Jeffrey to Pablo and back again. "Tell me about your case."

Jeffrey took a deep breath. "It's like this," he said, and he told her about the body they found, the killing at the hospital, and their trip to Monterey Park.

"The girl we saw at the hospital has high cheek bones and a very distinguishable face. I went online and found the yearbook for the high school in Monterey Park where we saw her. I went through every class, from freshman to senior, but I couldn't find her picture."

"Some people are uncomfortable about their looks," Marisol said. "They don't like having their picture in the yearbook."

"I know," Jeffrey said. "I'm that way myself."

"Trust me," said Pablo, "this girl has nothing to feel uncomfortable about."

Marisol shot a look at Pablo.

Jeffrey noticed and wondered if he saw a trace of jealousy in her eyes.

Pablo went on: "If she's not in that yearbook, it's not because of her looks, it's because she has something to hide."

"I was thinking the same thing," Jeffrey said. He reached for a folder on the coffee table and extracted a single page. "I did find this." He handed the page to Marisol.

Pablo sat on the sofa next to her and leaned in over her shoulder to see. The paper showed a picture of a high school bowling team, three boys and three girls, all Chinese.

Pablo pointed to one of the girls. "That looks like her."

Marisol ran her finger along the caption under the photo, which identified the six students by their first initial and last name. "Her name is C. Chan."

Pablo's looked up excitedly at Jeffrey. "Hey, she's related to Thomas Chan."

"Maybe," said Jeffrey. "Chan is a common Chinese name."

"Who's Thomas Chan?" asked Marisol.

"One of the guys that hit Jeffrey," said Pablo.

Marisol looked again at the caption under the photo. "They're all named Chan or Lee."

Jeffrey laughed. "Those are both common Chinese names. It's like an American named Smith or Anderson."

"Or Jones," said Marisol.

"Right."

"Your case does sound dangerous," Marisol said, "but I'll help if I can. What do you want me to do?"

"How's your Chinese?" Jeffrey asked her.

Marisol was fluent in English, Spanish and German, and she was currently studying Chinese. She held out her hand and flipped it back and forth. "It's okay. I know some mainland Chinese, but there are so many dialects."

"If you heard a conversation in Chinese, would you be able to understand what was being said?"

"Maybe."

"According to the yearbook, there's a bowling alley in Chinatown where they all practice. I was thinking about me and Pablo going there in these disguises to see if we can find anything."

"What about your parents?" Marisol asked. "Do they know?"

Jeffrey and Pablo shared a guilty look.

"Uh-oh," said Marisol.

"Here's the thing," Jeffrey said. He told her about their phone conversation with Eddie Lee, the possibility of a major crime occurring, and their theory that Kevin Wong was murdered at the hospital to keep him from talking.

"If some big crime is going to happen, we might be able to stop it. We might even save some people's lives."

"So you *are* lying to your parents."

"Hold on a second," Jeffrey said. "You make it sound like we're doing something awful."

"You are."

"We don't want to go against our parents," Pablo said, "but we feel like we have to. Jeffrey, tell her about the logic you came up with."

"Logic?" Marisol laughed. "So this is your idea, Jeffrey? And you talked Pablo into it?"

"I can think for myself," Pablo replied. "Tell her, Jeffrey."

Jeffrey cleared his throat. "Like Pablo said, we approached the situation from a position of logic. Suppose you were living in Communist Russia in the 1920s or 1930s when they were killing all the Christians ... and suppose you were hiding someone in your attic, and the Communists came around and asked you where that person was ... if you lied and told them you didn't know, would that be a sin?"

"No, it wouldn't be a sin," Marisol said, "but you're not hiding anyone in your attic."

"What if you were trying to escape Communist Russia in the 1930s," Pablo said, "and you had a fake passport and fake papers for you and your family, and the police asked if those were really your papers, and you lied and said, 'Yes,' would that be a sin?"

"But you're not trying to escape Communist Russia."

"Come on, Marisol. Don't you get what we're saying?"

"I get it, but it still seems kind of sneaky."

"It's sneaky, I agree," Jeffrey said. "But it boils down to doing something wrong in order to achieve something right."

"And you're doing that by lying to your parents."

"Technically, we're not lying," Jeffrey said. "We didn't say anything to them that isn't true."

"Technically, you are lying, because you're doing something that you know they don't want you to do, and you're sneaking around behind their backs."

"Now you're making me feel guilty."

"You should feel guilty."

"What if we don't do anything and somebody gets killed?" Pablo said.

"What if you do something and *you* get killed?" Marisol said.

"Like I said," Jeffrey told her. "We debated whether to ask you for help."

"I don't want to do anything sneaky or dishonest," Marisol said, "and neither should you. I can tell you exactly what's going to happen, Jeffrey. You're going to get deeper and deeper into this mystery, because you can't help yourself. And then, when it's too late, you're going to wish you hadn't. But by then you'll be in too much trouble."

Jeffrey and Pablo exchanged another guilty look.

"You see," Marisol said, "I know you, Jeffrey. I know exactly how that mind of yours works."

"This is all we're going to do," Jeffrey said. "Just this one little trip to Chinatown, and if we find anything, we'll give it to the police. And for you, none of this is sneaky or dishonest at all. Your mom didn't tell you not to investigate."

"And you're going along with this, Pablo?"

"I told you, I have a mind of my own."

Marisol sighed. "I'll help," she said, "but on one condition."

Jeffrey raised an eyebrow. "What's the condition?"

"Susie has to come too."

"No way," Jeffrey said. "Not her."

"Why not?"

"You know how I feel about Susie Norris. She's loud and obnoxious and above all, full of herself."

"That's what she says about you."

"*What?*"

"She says you're mean and selfish and above all, full of yourself."

Jeffrey's face flamed red. "Are you kidding me?"

"Well, that's what she says, but I don't know if she really means it. She's just mad, because you didn't want to dress up like Santa Claus for the children at her orphanage."

"I *did* dress up like Santa Claus," Jeffrey said, his nostrils flaring. "It was one of the most humiliating things I've ever done."

"Susie says she had to practically force you to do it, and then you left early."

"Well, how long did she want? She took a call on her phone and left me alone with all those brats."

"Jeffrey!"

"I'm serious." He shook his head. "No. No way. I mean it. Susie Norris is not going to be part of this investigation."

"Please, Jeffrey! Susie means well, she really does. She's just ... well, she's not very mature I guess you could say."

"That's the understatement of the year."

"But you see that's where you come in. You're mature, and you're smart, and you can be a good influence on her. A really good influence."

Jeffrey eyed her suspiciously. "Are you trying to con me?"

"A little."

Pablo laughed.

"Don't you see how perfect it would be?" Marisol said. "I mean, if I go, then it's two guys and a girl. People might wonder what we're up to. But if Susie goes, then it's two couples and no one will pay any attention to us."

Pablo turned to Jeffrey. "She has a point."

Jeffrey frowned. "Don't you have any other friends?"

"Of course, I do. But Susie is the best one for what you have in mind. Remember, she has her own phone. And if this case is as dangerous as you say it is, then we might need her to call for help in an emergency."

Jeffrey scowled. "Her and that phone."

Marisol cleared her throat. "I'm approaching the situation from a position of logic. And I know how much you appreciate logic."

Pablo nodded thoughtfully and turned to Jeffrey.

Jeffrey sighed.

"Then Susie can come?" Marisol asked.

Jeffrey shrugged and threw up his hands.

Marisol popped to her feet. "I'll call her right now." She ran to the kitchen. A moment later, the boys heard her speaking on the landline phone.

"Well, Jeffrey," Pablo said, "here we go again."

Chapter Seventeen – 5 Days Before Christmas

Susie stood on a Chinatown street corner and frowned up at the towering structures around her.

"I don't see a bowling alley," she said. "All I see are office buildings." She turned to Marisol. Marisol turned to Pablo. Pablo turned to Jeffrey.

Jeffrey glanced at an address written on a slip of paper in his hand. "This is the address." He nodded to a five-story office building across the street. "This has to be it." He and Pablo were dressed in their French disguises, and the girls did their best to imitate them. They wore jeans, turtleneck shirts and berets, with matching colored scarves around their necks.

Jeffrey led them to the building's entrance and pushed open the heavy glass door. A grim-faced Chinese man, dressed in a black jacket and tie, sat behind a guard desk in the center of the lobby. He eyed Jeffrey and his friends as they approached.

"Excusez moi," Jeffrey said. "piste de bowling?"

The man narrowed his eyes. "Bowling?"

"Oui."

The man held up his hand and spread his five fingers apart.

"Merci."

Jeffrey and his friends went to the elevator and took it up to the fifth floor.

As the elevator door opened, the smell of floor wax wafted in, and they heard the crack of a marble bowling ball as it struck across pins and sent them clattering in their cage. It was followed by shouts of glee and then the sound of another bowling ball striking pins.

They stepped out of the elevator and onto a small terrace. The terrace was lined with clothing and cosmetic shops and it stretched around an open floor. The bowling alley was one floor below and accessible only by an escalator. Jeffrey and his friends stood at a rail on the terrace and gazed down upon a crowd of Asian teens and young adults.

"This is the strangest thing," Susie said.

Marisol nodded. "From the outside, you would never guess there was a bowling alley in here."

"It's like a secret club or something," Pablo said.

"Before we start investigating," Jeffrey said, "let's find all the exits. We might have to make a fast getaway."

He led them on a complete circle of the terrace, noting the locations of two emergency stairwells, and then they returned to where they started and leaned against the rail.

Jeffrey's eyes scanned the crowd below them in the bowling alley. A cluster of Chinese teens behind one of the bowling lanes caught his attention. They were dressed identically in blue jeans and orange striped shirts, and they were gathered around someone, who was seated in front of them. The group parted and walked away and Jeffrey saw the object of their attention.

"That's her," he whispered.

The others looked. The girl named C. Chan sat by herself, as if she were waiting for someone. She was dressed in the same jeans and orange striped shirt as the others.

"She's pretty," Susie said.

"She's an accomplice to murder," Jeffrey said. "Or so I think."

Pablo tapped Jeffrey on the arm and nodded towards the far end of the bowling alley. Jeffrey looked and saw Thomas Chan walking behind the row of bowling lanes. With him was the boy with the red headband and the driver of the black Mercedes that Jeffrey and Pablo encountered in Monterey Park. Jeffrey felt his body tensing.

"What is it?" Susie asked.

"Those are the guys that jumped me and Jeffrey," Pablo said.

Marisol gasped. "Let's get out of here."

"Hold on a second," Jeffrey said. "They can't possibly see us up here."

Thomas and his two cohorts continued walking past the crowd of younger teens.

"He's going straight to the girl," Pablo said.

The girl saw Thomas approaching and sat up straight. Thomas and his friends stopped in front of her.

"I would love to know what they're saying," Jeffrey said. "It might be the key to the whole case." He turned to Marisol. "Are you up for it?"

The color drained from Marisol's face. "Sure," she said.

"You don't have to."

"It's okay. I'll go. That's why we're here, right?"

Pablo reached for her arm. "I'll go with you," he said.

Susie watched as Pablo walked with Marisol to the escalator.

"Pablo's going with Marisol to protect her," she said. "How romantic."

Jeffrey felt his face flush hot. He waited for the heat to drain and said, "Standby with that phone of yours. Be ready to call the police."

Susie slid her fingers into the back pocket of her jeans and pulled out her phone.

Jeffrey turned back to the rail and watched. Thomas was standing directly in front of the girl and gesturing wildly with his arms. She sat stoically, watching him and listening. Behind them, Pablo and Marisol strolled by and stopped. Pablo stooped down and pretended to tie his shoe.

The girl said something to Thomas, and a moment later, she suddenly rose angrily from her seat and walked away. Thomas appeared to call after her, but she ignored him and continued walking. Thomas threw up his hands and he and his two friends went off in the opposite direction of the girl.

Pablo and Marisol walked briskly back to the escalator. As they reached the fifth floor, Marisol ran ahead and stopped in front of Jeffrey, full of importance with the news that she brought.

"Some of it I couldn't understand," she said, "but I heard him say, 'Everything's set for Sunday night.' Then she said, 'I'm not going.' He said, 'You have to go. He wants you there.' Then she said something I didn't understand, and he said, 'I do what he tells me to do.' And then she got up and walked away."

"What do you think it means, Jeffrey?" asked Pablo. "It doesn't sound like a gang war."

"No, not at all," said Jeffrey. He furrowed his brow in thought. "Whatever it is, there's somebody big calling the shots."

"She was really mad about something," Marisol said.

"Yeah, I saw that," Jeffrey said.

"Could it be another murder they're planning?" Pablo asked.

Jeffrey opened his mouth to speak, but was interrupted by a squawk of horror coming from Susie. "They see us," she cried.

Jeffrey looked down at the bowling alley below. The security guard from the lobby stood next to Thomas and his two friends. The guard lifted his arm and pointed directly up at Jeffrey.

Jeffrey and his friends backed away from the rail.

"We're in trouble now," Pablo said. "If we take the elevator, they'll be waiting for us."

"We'll take the emergency stairwell," Jeffrey said.

They hurried towards it. Susie glanced over her shoulder. "They're coming up the escalator."

Jeffrey pushed open the stairwell door and they clattered down the steps, past the landing on the fourth floor. A door opened two floors below them. A second security guard, dressed in a black jacket and tie, stepped through the open door and looked up the stairwell.

Jeffrey and his friends stopped and reversed course, heading back up the stairs. Pablo pulled open the door on the fourth floor landing. The others followed him through. They were in the back of the bowling alley.

Jeffrey led them towards the crowded bowling lanes. "They won't try anything here in front of all these witnesses," he said. "At least, I hope not."

"Here they come," Marisol said.

Jeffrey turned to see Thomas and his two cohorts walking through the crowd in their direction. The security guard from the lobby was with them. Jeffrey and Pablo stood side by side and faced the approaching party. Marisol and Susie filled in behind them. Jeffrey whispered over his shoulder, "Susie, if anything happens, call the police."

"Right," she said.

Thomas and his friends stopped in front of them.

Jeffrey smiled wide. "Bonjour! Comment allez-vous?"

Thomas stared back at him, angry and grim-faced. "Cut the crap," he said. He motioned at Pablo and the two girls. "You stay here. You," he crooked his finger at Jeffrey, "come with me. There's somebody here who wants to talk to you."

For a moment, nobody moved.

"Now," said Thomas.

"Don't go, Jeffrey," Marisol whispered.

Pablo glanced at the four adversaries in front of them and slowly curled his right hand into a fist. The boy in the red head-band seemed to read Pablo's thoughts. He drew back his jacket to reveal a gun tucked into the waistband of his pants.

"Don't even think about it," he said.

Jeffrey felt his heart thudding loudly against his chest. ""Excusez moi," he said to his friends, and took a step forward.

Thomas pointed ahead. "Walk straight." Jeffrey obeyed and Thomas followed. The boy in the red headband, the driver of the Mercedes, and the guard from the lobby remained with Pablo and the two girls.

Jeffrey kept walking.

"Turn right," Thomas commanded.

Jeffrey obeyed.

"Up the stairs."

Jeffrey climbed three short steps and found himself in a small restaurant, hidden in the back recesses of the building. The strong scent of incense opened his nose, followed by the smell of rice and chicken dumplings.

"Walk to the back," Thomas said.

The lighting was dim. Jeffrey slowed his walk so he could see where he was going. He passed tables of elderly Chinese men and women, loudly slurping soup.

Ahead of Jeffrey, a solitary table waited. A Chinese man dressed in a black T-shirt and jacket and wearing dark glasses sat alone at the table, facing him. The man remained motionless as Jeffrey approached.

"Sit down," Thomas said.

Jeffrey sat at the table, across from the man.

Thomas circled the table and stood behind the man's right shoulder.

The man turned his head to the left and barked a command in Chinese. From the shadows behind him, the girl, C. Chan, emerged. She approached the table with a folder in her hand.

Jeffrey felt his eyes widening. Seeing her up close, she looked even prettier than before, with smooth, flawless skin and a lower lip that protruded ever so slightly.

The girl seemed to sense Jeffrey's attention. She kept her eyes down, refusing to look his way. She handed the folder to the man and stepped back, standing behind his left shoulder.

The man removed his dark glasses and Jeffrey felt an urge to leap out of his chair. The man had the same flat face as Thomas, but his right eye was completely gouged out, leaving only a hollow hole in its place. The man's one good eye was glazed over with an ugly yellow tint. It was the man that Eddie Lee had told him about: Thomas Chan's father.

The one-eyed man opened the folder, glanced at the contents and grunted. He closed the folder and tossed it on the table in front of Jeffrey.

"That's you, isn't it?" he said.

Jeffrey opened the folder. Inside were dozens of news stories printed off the internet about him and Pablo, detailing their first case when they helped free Marisol's brother from jail and their second case when they found a treasure worth two hundred million dollars. Jeffrey glanced at only the first couple of clippings and nodded.

The man reached across the table, took the folder back and handed it to the girl.

"So your name is Jeffrey Jones?" he said.

"Yes."

"Now that we know who you are, perhaps you'll remove that ridiculous disguise."

Jeffrey slumped in his seat, too deflated to meet the man's gaze. He reached for the black beret atop his head and dropped it on the table in front of him. He did the same with the shades over his eyeglasses, unclipping them and dropping them on top of the beret. Using his index finger, he scratched at the tip of his fake mustache and when the corner lifted, he peeled it slowly away from the space over his upper lip. Holding the mustache between his thumb and index finger, he dropped it on the table.

The one-eyed man studied him. "Do not feel ashamed, my friend. Your disguise was actually quite clever. What gave you away was your stomach."

Thomas grinned. "You couldn't hide that, could you, fat boy?"

"Enough," snapped the one-eyed man. He turned back to Jeffrey. "Obesity is quite common in your country. Your women are particularly revolting. They have no respect for themselves."

Thomas grinned again. "They're all fat."

The man slapped the table with his hand and turned to Thomas. "Enough, I said." He faced Jeffrey. "Not only are your women obese, they put tattoos on their skin, and rings in their noses, and colored dyes in their hair. They resemble animals at the zoo. Most Asian women are not that way. You will find they remain slender and graceful throughout their lives. When the time is appropriate," he said in a low, conspiratorial voice, "I suggest you marry a nice Chinese girl."

Jeffrey felt his face reddening. He glanced at C. Chan. She blushed and lowered her eyes.

The man leaned back in his chair. "And now you will tell me why you are spying on me."

"I'm not."

The man stared back at him. His yellow-tinged eye seemed to bore its way into Jeffrey's brain. Jeffrey felt flustered and blurted out, "How can I be spying on you when I don't even know who you are?"

"I will ask the questions here, not you. Perhaps you don't know me, but I know you. Why did you feel the need to camouflage your appearance and what did you come here to find?"

"I'm investigating a murder."

"Whose murder?"

"A Chinese man that was killed at the county hospital."

"What is this man's name?"

"Kevin Wong."

"And who hired you to conduct this investigation?"

"No one."

The man frowned. He reached into the inside breast pocket of his jacket and removed a pearl handle, six inches long. He held the object in his right hand for Jeffrey to see. "Do you know what this is?"

Jeffrey shook his head.

The man pressed a lever with his thumb and a five inch steel blade flicked out from the handle and locked into place.

"Now do you know?" the man said.

Jeffrey eyed the glistening steel of the switchblade knife. "Yes sir."

"Then perhaps you will stop lying and tell me the truth. Who hired you to investigate this dead man?"

"Nobody hired me," Jeffrey said.

A look of fury flashed across the man's face. The knife in his right hand switched deftly to an overhand grip. His left arm swept across the table, clearing it of Jeffrey's disguise. His right arm raised high and swooped down. The knife whistled through the air and shunked into the center of the wooden table. Thomas and C. Chan stepped back with alarm.

"I want the truth," the man demanded.

"That is the truth!"

"Why is this dead Chinese man of interest to you?"

"I found him shot-up and lying in some lady's backyard. I felt responsible for him."

"But now he is dead, a low-life petty criminal. So why do you care?"

"Murder is murder."

The man spread his arms wide. "And what did you expect to find here?"

Jeffrey squirmed.

"Answer me," the man insisted.

Jeffrey nodded reluctantly at the girl. "I was following her."

C. Chan stared back at Jeffrey.

"Why?" the man asked.

"She was at the hospital when the murder took place."

"And that makes her guilty?"

"It makes her a person of interest."

The man gestured at C. Chan. "So now she is here. Ask her what you want."

Jeffrey hesitated.

The man was insistent. "You followed her, you found her. So ask her."

The girl stood rigid.

Jeffrey straightened his glasses and cleared his throat. "Why were you at the hospital that day?"

The girl's voice was smooth and soft. "Kevin Wong worked for my uncle." She gestured towards the one-eyed man. "I was concerned."

"Why did you go down the stairs instead of the elevator?"

"I was sad. I wanted to be alone."

"Did you prop open the doors in the stairwell at the hospital so the killer could have access?"

"No."

Jeffrey fixed her with an incriminating stare. "Are you an accessory to murder?"

The girl stared back at him for a long moment.

"No," she said.

"Finished?" the one-eyed man asked.

Jeffrey nodded.

The man reached for his knife. The blue veins on his wrist quivered and bulged as he pulled on the handle. The knife moved slowly upward and pulled free from the table with a sucking sound. The man removed a handkerchief from his pocket and wiped the blade clean.

"Imagine taking that in the heart," he said with a chuckle.

He pressed the button and the blade retracted back into the handle. He pocketed the knife. "I don't know if I can believe you," he said to Jeffrey.

"It's the truth," Jeffrey said.

The man turned and looked over his right shoulder at Thomas. "Do you believe him?"

Thomas shook his head. "Not a word."

The man turned to his left and faced the girl. "Clarisse?"

Jeffrey's ears perked up. So that was her name – Clarisse.

She studied Jeffrey for a long moment.

"Yes, I believe him," she said.

Chapter Eighteen

"They're up to something," Jeffrey said. "I don't know what."

He stood on a street corner in Chinatown with his friends, waiting for the bus to take them home.

"Counterfeiting or murder?" Pablo asked.

"Probably both," Jeffrey answered. "But then it doesn't make sense why they would let us go."

"I have an idea," Marisol said. The others turned to her. "Jeffrey, you said there was some kind of crime being planned; something so big that they had to kill that guy at the hospital to shut him up."

"Right," Jeffrey nodded.

"Well then that's why they let us go. If they did anything to us now, it would attract too much attention."

Susie snapped her fingers. "And whatever the crime is, it's probably going to take place on Sunday night, like Marisol heard them talking."

"That's only three days from now," Pablo said. "What do you think it could be, Jeffrey?"

Jeffrey shook his head. "I don't know, but I'm starting to feel guilty about this whole case."

"You see!" Marisol said. "I told you."

"You were right, Marisol," Jeffrey admitted. "We shouldn't be sneaking around like this. I feel awful. Plus, this whole case is getting too dangerous. I hate to give up, but I vote we go to the police, give them all the information we have, and then let them deal with it."

"We're quitting the case?" Pablo asked.

Before Jeffrey could answer, a lumbering city bus pulled up to the curb and the door swooshed open. The boys stepped aside to let Marisol and Susie on first. As Susie started to board the bus, a girl's voice called out behind them, "Wait!"

Jeffrey and his friends turned to see Clarisse striding up the sidewalk towards them. "Please, wait," she said.

Susie stepped down from the bus. It pulled away from the curb and drove off.

Clarisse nodded at Jeffrey, and then to the others. "I want to apologize. My cousin and his friends and my uncle, they were all very rude. Please, I don't want you to get the wrong idea."

"What's the wrong idea?" Jeffrey asked.

"That my uncle and his son are some kind of criminals."

"Aren't they?"

"No! Not at all." Clarisse touched her nose lightly. "The reason they are so suspicious of you is because they think you are spies."

"*Spies?*" said Pablo.

Clarisse nodded. "In China, corporate espionage is big business."

"Do we look like Chinese spies?" Pablo asked.

"No, you do not. But Chinese businesses and the government often use children as covers or spies. I know you're not children;

you're the same age as me, but that only made my uncle more suspicious. He thought you were spying on his business."

"What kind of business is your uncle in?" Jeffrey asked.

"Printing." Clarisse rubbed the side of her nose.

"Are there secrets worth stealing in the printing business?"

"You'd be surprised. Every business has secrets worth stealing." She touched Jeffrey lightly on the arm. "Please, come to our house." She motioned to the others. "All of you. My cousin will drive us. My uncle knows he made a mistake and he feels bad."

Jeffrey glanced at his friends. Pablo's eyes were hopeful. Susie's eyes were curious. Marisol's eyes were suspicious. "Sure," Jeffrey said, and he caught Marisol's disapproving look.

Clarisse turned to the girls and extended her hand. "My name is Clarisse." Marisol and Susie shook hands with Clarisse and introduced themselves. Clarisse led the girls down the sidewalk. The boys followed.

Pablo sidled up to Jeffrey and whispered: "You've got that look, Jeffrey. What's on your mind?"

Jeffrey whispered back: "Did you see the way she touched her nose while she was talking?"

Pablo thought for a moment and nodded. "Yeah. So?"

"When a person tells a lie their heart pumps faster and it makes the nose swell and itch. It's called the Pinocchio effect."

"You mean that's real?"

"To an extent. When a person touches their nose or their face while they're talking, it's usually a sign they're not telling the truth."

Pablo's eyes grew wide. "Do you think she's lying?"

Jeffrey didn't hesitate. "I know she's lying."

"This place is huge," Pablo exclaimed.

He stood with Jeffrey, Clarisse, Marisol and Susie outside a majestic estate in Monterey Park. "Who lives here, if you don't mind my asking?"

"Myself and my uncle," Clarisse said. She led them up the walk, past a landscaped front yard. Flowers of all colors bloomed in patches around the yard and surrounded a bubbling fountain. Aside from the happy chirping of birds, the street was silent.

"That's it?" Pablo said. "Just the two of you?"

Clarisse nodded sheepishly. "Mainly just me. My uncle is often away on business."

She stopped before the front door and removed her shoes. Her toenails, painted purple like her fingernails, peaked out from under the hem of her jeans. Marisol and Susie noticed self-consciously. Clarisse placed her shoes next to a long line of other shoes to the right of the front door. The others saw her, removed their own shoes and placed them next to hers. Clarisse unlocked the front door and led them all inside.

The marble floor of the entrance hall was cold under their feet. A Cocker Spaniel puppy appeared at the far end of the hall and scampered towards Clarisse.

"Hello, Doodle," Clarisse said.

Pablo raised an eyebrow. "Doodle?"

"That's his name." Clarisse kneeled beside the pup and embraced it. "You love me, don't you, Doodle?"

The pup barked.

"What kind of a name is Doodle?" asked Pablo.

"It goes with his siblings: Yankee and Dandy."

As if on cue, two more puppies appeared and bounded down the hall to Clarisse.

"Yankee, Doodle and Dandy," said Susie. "How cute."

"It's my uncle's favorite American movie," Clarisse said. "The only one he'll watch."

The three pups leapt about Clarisse, tails wagging furiously. Clarisse embraced the three of them together, pulled their little bodies against hers, and closed her eyes.

Jeffrey studied her. Alone in the big house, with only the three dogs to keep her company, she struck him as the loneliest girl he'd ever seen.

Marisol and Susie bent down to pet the pups.

Pablo stepped towards a large window at the rear of the house. Outside the window, was a swimming pool. Steam rose from the shimmering water.

"You have a pool?" Pablo said.

Clarisse opened her eyes, released the puppies, and stood up. "You're welcome to use it. It's heated."

"Seriously?" Pablo said. "We can go swimming?"

"If you wish. There are bathing suits and towels in the guest changing rooms."

Pablo stared out the window at the sparkling blue water. "We can go swimming, five days before Christmas," he said.

"How often do you go swimming, Clarisse?" Marisol asked.

"Never."

Four surprised faces turned her way.

"Never?" said Marisol.

"Never." Clarisse waved to a sunken living room to their right. "Please, sit down. I'll make tea."

The four friends started towards the living room, followed by the pups.

"Jeffrey."

It was Clarisse's voice.

Jeffrey stopped and faced her. He liked hearing her use his name.

"Perhaps you can help me," she said.

"Sure," he said, and followed her into the kitchen.

"What a gentleman," Susie called after him, her voice dripping with sarcasm.

"Shhh," Pablo whispered. "She might talk more freely if she's alone with Jeffrey."

Marisol gave him a sour look. "I thought we were dropping the case."

"We are," Pablo said. "I mean, we will. Only we can't pass this up."

Like the rest of the house, the kitchen was huge. Jeffrey had never seen a kitchen that big in his life.

Clarisse reached for a tea kettle and rinsed it in the sink. She glanced over her shoulder at Jeffrey. "I looked through that file that my uncle has on you. You seem to help people. Like you helped that boy who was arrested and went to jail for something he didn't do."

"That was Marisol's brother," Jeffrey said.

"So you *do* help people?"

"I try to help, when I can. *If* I can."

Clarisse finished rinsing the tea kettle and set it on the counter. She turned and faced him, but said nothing. Her expression was stoic.

"Do you need help?" Jeffrey asked her.

The girl said nothing.

"Is your uncle involved in some kind of crime?" Jeffrey asked.

Clarisse cast her eyes downward and paused for a long moment. Finally, she said, "He's not my uncle."

"I don't understand."

"He's not my uncle – not my blood uncle."

"Then who is he, and where are your parents?"

"My parents are dead. They were killed for protesting the government in China."

"Who's that guy with one eye?"

Clarisse turned away from him

"It's complicated," she said, and opened a cabinet door.

"The truth is never complicated," Jeffrey said. "Neither is right or wrong. Or Heaven and hell."

Clarisse removed a pair of tea cups from the cabinet. "What do you mean Heaven and hell?" She set the cups on the table.

"I mean you're either on your way to Heaven or you're on your way to hell. There's no middle ground."

Clarisse reached for another tea cup from the cabinet. Jeffrey noticed her hand trembling and said, "If you're somehow involved in a murder or counterfeiting, then you're on your way to hell."

Clarisse flinched and dropped the cup. It hit the floor and shattered into a dozen pieces. Clarisse raised a startled hand to her mouth.

Pablo's voice called from the living room, "Everything okay in there?"

"We're fine," Jeffrey called back. He waved at Clarisse to stand still. "Careful, you'll cut yourself."

Clarisse stepped back. "I'm not involved," she snapped. "I told you that at the bowling alley."

"You asked about my helping people," Jeffrey said. "If you need help, let me know." He reached for the waste basket and pulled it close. The two of them got down on their knees and gingerly picked up the broken pieces.

"In China we are taught atheism," Clarisse said, and dropped a piece from the broken cup into the waste basket. "They tell us there is no God."

"That's the dumbest thing I ever heard."

Her face reddened and anger flashed in her eyes. "You can't prove that God is real."

"Sure, you can."

"How?"

"Evidence."

"I'm not talking about your Bible book."

"I'm not either." He picked up a piece from the broken cup and dropped it in the waste basket.

"Then what is your evidence?" Clarisse asked.

"The Shroud of Turin is a good place to start. It's Jesus's burial cloth and it has his picture on it. That's hard physical evidence. Our Lady of Guadalupe is another. In 1531, the mother of Jesus appeared to a peasant in Mexico and imprinted her image on his cloak. The cloak is made of cactus fiber and should have deteriorated after twenty years, but it still exists in good condition five hundred years later. You can go look at it yourself. It's hanging on the wall in a church in Mexico. That's more hard physical evidence."

Jeffrey picked up another piece of the broken cup. "And In 1917, the mother of Jesus appeared to three kids in Portugal. To prove she was real, she made the sun dance and spin in the sky in front of seventy-thousand people. That's eye-witness evidence. All the newspapers reported it, even the Communist ones. In fact, the Communist newspapers sent reporters there to make fun of it. They said it was all a hoax. But then it actually happened and they were forced to report it."

"How is that possible?"

"It was a miracle. There's no other explanation. There's a lot more. There are stories of saints raising people from the dead in order to baptize them, or priests performing miracle cures, or saints who are dead, but their bodies haven't decomposed."

"That's impossible!"

"Look it up." He deposited the last broken piece of cup in the waste basket and he and Clarisse rose to their feet.

"Have you read any Sherlock Holmes stories?" Jeffrey asked.

Clarisse shook her head.

"Sherlock Holmes is a famous fictional detective," Jeffrey explained. "He used to say, 'When you eliminate the impossible, all that remains, no matter how improbable, must be the truth.' That evidence I just told you about, when you eliminate the impossible – that man could have done them himself – all that remains is divine intervention, or proof of God. That's why I say I'm an evidence guy. Facts and evidence are real, whether people believe them or not."

"I never heard of those things you said."

"That's because nobody wants you to know. They want to drag you down to hell where they're going."

"How do I know you're not lying?"

Jeffrey shrugged. "I have no reason to."

"And these things are real?"

"Sure. You can look them up for yourself on the internet or at the library. Look up Our Lady of Guadalupe, the Shroud of Turin, and Our Lady of Fatima, and then tell me if I'm lying."

"Is Heaven real?"

"Sure, it's real."

"And what is Heaven?"

"Heaven is a place of beauty, love and happiness. But very few people actually make it there."

Clarisse leaned against the counter and stared down at the sink.

"What is hell?" she asked quietly.

"Hell is a place of unending torment, where people burn in flames for all eternity."

"And this is forever?"

Jeffrey nodded. "Forever and ever."

"Who goes there?"

"Almost everyone."

Clarisse faced him. "What do you mean 'everyone'?"

"I mean, maybe one percent of the population goes to Heaven. Maybe. The rest all end up in hell."

"Why do you say that?"

"Because I study human nature. People are stupid. People are weak. And almost everyone is going to hell."

Clarisse frowned. "How can you say that everyone is bad?"

"I didn't say they were bad, I said they were stupid and weak. They're being led astray be people who actually are bad. People who reject Jesus, or people who commit sins like murder, abortion and stealing are all going to hell when they die."

Clarisse stood silently for a long moment, staring down at the floor. "There's something I need to tell you," she said, "but I am afraid."

"You don't have to be afraid."

She turned away from him.

Jeffrey watched her. "Why don't you start by telling me what's going to happen on Sunday night?"

Clarisse spun around to face him, her eyes filled with fear. "Who told you about that?"

"Clarisse!"

It was the voice of the one-eyed man. They heard his footsteps outside and then the kitchen door opened and he stepped into the room. He saw Jeffrey and smiled wide. "Welcome, my friend. Clarisse has explained to you about our misunderstanding?"

Jeffrey nodded.

"Excellent," the man said. "Then we can all be friends and put this nonsense behind us." He extended his hand and he and Jeffrey shook.

Jeffrey glanced at Clarisse. She stared back at him. Slowly, almost imperceptibly, she shook her head 'no.'

Chapter Nineteen – 4 Days Before Christmas

"I don't want Grandma to see me like this," Jeffrey said, pointing at his face. He stood in the kitchen, dressed in the rumpled sweat pants and T-shirt that he slept in.

His mother sat at the kitchen table, signing Christmas cards. Her laptop was open on the table beside her and from it came the voice of Burl Ives singing *A Holly Jolly Christmas.*

Jeffrey's father knelt before a large wooden bookcase, wiping it down with a clean towel. A large red ribbon with a red bow on top encircled the bookcase. The warm smell of bacon and eggs from his parents' breakfast remained in the air.

"Too bad," said Jeffrey's father. "You should have thought of that before you went snooping after that girl in Monterey Park."

"I mean it, Dad."

"I mean it, too. Now get dressed."

"Actually, Jeffrey has a point," his mother said. She signed her name on a Christmas card with a flourish and offered her pen to Jeffrey. "Sign Grandma's card."

Jeffrey took the pen, bent over the kitchen table and signed the card. His mother twisted around in her chair and faced her husband. "You know how your mother is. She faints at the sight of blood. One look at Jeffrey with all those bruises and she's liable to have a heart attack."

Jeffrey's father sighed and rose to his feet. "Come here," he said, and motioned at Jeffrey to step forward.

Jeffrey stepped tentatively towards his father.

"Take off your glasses."

Jeffrey removed his glasses. His father placed a hand on either side of Jeffrey's head and tilted his face left and right, inspecting his bruises. "It's been ten days. Your face is actually a lot better. I can see most of the swelling has gone down." He released Jeffrey. "But you're still a mess."

"Thanks a lot."

"You want an honest appraisal, don't you?"

Jeffrey's mother placed a Christmas card inside an envelope, licked the envelope flap and sealed it. "Jeffrey, your grandmother is going to be very disappointed if you don't come with us."

"I'll see her in a few days for Christmas dinner. By then I should look halfway normal."

"Your breakfast is in the oven. I kept it warm for you. Other than that, there's no food here," said his mother, "only leftovers from last night."

"Leftovers are fine."

"You look thinner. Have you lost weight?"

Jeffrey froze. Maybe all those skipped lunches *had* made him lose weight.

"Have you?" his mother asked.

"I don't think so," he said, without elaboration. He didn't want his parents to know that he spent his lunch periods alone, hiding in the library.

"Maybe it's those bruises. They make you look thinner."

His father slapped his hand atop the bookcase. "Give me a hand with this thing, kid." He opened the back door and he and Jeffrey lifted the bookcase and carried it outside.

They carried the bookcase around the house to the family car, waiting in the driveway.

"I'm glad you came to your senses and dropped this whole detective thing," said Jeffrey's father as they lowered the bookcase onto the concrete driveway. "Your mother and I sleep much easier at night."

Jeffrey looked his father in the eye and nodded. Everything Marisol had said was right. He made up his mind then and there that he was dropping the case. He would turn in what he knew to the two homicide detectives and that would be it.

"We'll be home tomorrow," his father said. "You want to hang out with Pablo, fine. Otherwise stay home."

"Right," Jeffrey said.

His father smiled and clapped him on the shoulder. "I'm proud of you."

Jeffrey forced himself to smile. He felt bad for putting on this show, but he knew that if he flinched in any way it would telegraph his guilt, so he kept his eyes fixed on his father and a stupid half-smile plastered across his face, feeling worse and worse with each passing second.

After his parents left, Jeffrey wasted no time. He called Pablo and explained how he felt. Pablo told Jeffrey he felt the same way and they agreed to go the police together. An hour later they were seated before the two police detectives in Wolfe's office.

"I thought I told both of you to mind your own business," Wolfe said.

"We are," Jeffrey replied. "We're through with everything, both of us." He motioned at Pablo with his hand and Pablo nodded.

"Then why are you here?" Wolfe asked.

"I'm giving you what we have," Jeffrey said. "You can take it from there. First off, I was assaulted in Monterey Park by a gang member named Thomas Chan. I want to press charges." He reached in his shirt pocket and removed a slip of paper. "Here's his name and address." He offered the paper to the two men, but neither took it.

Wolfe shrugged and leaned back in this chair. "You'll have to press charges at the front desk. We're homicide detectives."

Jeffrey looked at Ratburn. The man smiled and said nothing.

"Fine," Jeffrey said. "We'll press charges downstairs. But that's not all." He reached in his pocket and removed the yearbook photo of Clarisse with the school bowling team. "This is the girl I saw at the hospital." He handed the photo to Wolfe. "The one who propped the doors open in the stairwell so the killer could enter the hospital quietly. Her name is Clarisse Chan. For what it's worth, I think she's caught up in this whole mess involuntarily."

Wolfe stared at the photo, and the color drained from his face. "Where did you get this?"

"On the internet. It's from her yearbook. You can see her initial and last name underneath the picture. She's related to Thomas Chan, I think."

"You *think?*"

"I'm not entirely certain. Thomas Chan's father, is involved in this too. He's a Chinese man with one eye."

"A man with one eye?" said Ratburn.

"That's right."

"And what are we supposed to do with this?" Wolfe asked, waving the photo.

"I recommend you question her about the murder at the hospital."

Ratburn leaned forward with a look of disbelief. "You recommend we question a murder suspect?"

"That's right," Jeffrey said.

"We recommend you do it quickly," Pablo added.

Ratburn turned to Wolfe and pointed his thumb back at the boys. "Can you believe these two?"

Wolfe kept his eyes fixed on Pablo. "Why do you recommend we do it quickly?"

"Because there's another crime planned for this Sunday night," Pablo said, "and it could be another murder."

Both men stared hard at the boys.

"What kind of crime are you talking about?" said Wolfe.

"We don't know," Jeffrey said. "But we suspect it's something big. It could involve counterfeiting or it could involve murder."

"Or it could involve both," Pablo said.

Neither man spoke for a long moment. Finally, Wolfe said, "Where are your parents?"

"Visiting my grandma," Jeffrey said. "They'll be home tomorrow."

Wolfe turned to Pablo. "And yours?"

"My dad's at work," Pablo said. "My mom's out Christmas shopping."

"Okay," Wolfe said with a sigh. "We'll investigate it. Thanks."

Jeffrey stared at the two men. He wasn't expecting their meeting to end so quickly.

"Go home, kid," said Ratburn.

The two boys rose and walked to the door. Ratburn called after them, "How old are you, boy?"

Jeffrey paused at the door. "Fifteen."

"Shouldn't you be playing video games, or chasing girls, or something?"

"I am chasing girls," Jeffrey said. He nodded at the photo in Wolfe's hand. "And there she is."

He opened the door and he and Pablo stepped out.

Ratburn sprang out of his chair and slammed the door shut behind them. He turned to his partner. Wolfe lifted his hand to his neck and made a slashing motion across his throat.

Jeffrey was rifling through the refrigerator, looking for the leftovers his mother had mentioned when the phone rang. He checked the caller ID and saw the name Susie Norris. Jeffrey cringed. Why was she calling him? Didn't she know he hated her? She was the last person he wanted to talk to.

He decided to let the call go to voicemail, but quickly changed his mind. His parents might be able to retrieve the message even if he erased it, and the message might be something that would get him in trouble. Besides, he didn't want them knowing that a girl had called him. He snatched up the phone and heard Pablo's voice.

"I'm glad it's you," Jeffrey said with surprise. "What are you doing on Susie's phone?"

"Just hanging out at my house. Listen, I'm doing alright. Nothing great, everything real. Can you come over?"

Jeffrey hesitated. He and Pablo had left the police station three hours ago. Pablo seemed fine then, but now his voice sounded strained, and why was Susie at his house? He heard a muffled voice on the other end.

Jeffrey pressed the phone tighter against his ear. "Pablo? You still there?"

The line went dead.

Jeffrey checked the caller ID for Susie's phone number and called it. The line rang four times and then went to her voicemail. Jeffrey hung up. Something strange was afoot, but he didn't know what. He called Pablo's house.

Mrs. Reyes answered the phone. She sounded surprised when Jeffrey asked to speak with Pablo. "He's not with you? He told me he was going to your house."

"I saw him this morning," Jeffrey said, "but I haven't seen him since then. He just called me from Susie's phone."

"Susie Norris?"

"Yeah."

"What's he doing on her phone?"

"I don't know. He told me she was with him at your house."

"He told you Susie Norris was here at our house?"

"Yeah."

"Now I'm worried," said Mrs. Reyes.

"Maybe it's some kind of joke," Jeffrey told her.

"I don't care. This is unusual for him. Pablo doesn't play jokes like that. I'm calling Susie's mother. I'll call you later."

Jeffrey hung up. Something was definitely wrong. Should he call Pablo's mother back and tell her about the case and their trip to the police station? The phone rang, interrupting his thoughts.

The caller ID showed Father Pat's name. Jeffrey answered quickly.

The voice on the line was shaky. "Are you sitting down?"

"No, Father. Should I be?"

He heard a whimpering cry from the elderly priest and then the words, "Eddie Lee is dead."

Jeffrey froze. "What happened?"

"He was murdered; stabbed in the back over a dozen times. I just found out."

Father Pat kept talking, but Jeffrey didn't hear a word. His mind swirled with the realization that he was responsible for a man's death. And if Eddie Lee was dead, who was next? He leaned heavily against the kitchen counter to keep from falling. Finally, he heard Father Pat say, "I have to go. His family is coming here to discuss his funeral," and the line clicked off.

Jeffrey's heart began to pound. Everything was closing in fast.

Where was Pablo?

He called Susie's number again. No answer.

He grabbed a piece of paper and a pen and sat down at the kitchen table. Quickly, he wrote down everything he remembered from his short phone conversation with Pablo. Eight words caught his attention: *Listen, I'm doing alright. Nothing great, everything real.*

Jeffrey had never heard Pablo use the expression *nothing great, everything real*. In fact, he'd never heard those words before from anybody. What did they mean?

Pablo had even prefaced the sentence with the word *listen*, like he wanted Jeffrey to pay close attention to what he was about to say.

Was Pablo in trouble? If so, he'd have to act fast. On a hunch, Jeffrey wrote Pablo's words in a column:

Listen
I'm
Doing
Alright
Nothing
Great
Everything
Real

Jeffrey stared at the words, his heart racing. What was Pablo trying to tell him?

Suddenly, it jumped out at him. The first letter of each the last six words spelled DANGER.

Jeffrey shot to his feet. His stomach jolted the table and his chair tipped back and clattered to the tile floor.

He rushed to the phone and paused, his hand resting on the receiver. If he called the police, what would he tell them? That a friend of his had called with a coded message about some kind of unnamed danger? They'd laugh at him and hang up. Or worse, they'd send the guys in the white coats over to take him away. The phone rang, startling him.

The caller ID read *Susie Norris*.

Jeffrey snatched up the phone. "Hello?"

There was silence on the line.

"Hello!" Jeffrey shouted.

The line clicked dead.

Jeffrey hung up. Eddie Lee was dead, Pablo was in danger, and he was alone in the house. From the entrance hall came the sound of heavy fists pounding on the front door.

Jeffrey's heart jumped. He ran from the kitchen to the entrance hall. The pounding continued. The heavy oak door shook on its hinges.

"Who is it?" Jeffrey yelled.

A voice outside the door shouted, "Police! Open up!"

Jeffrey stepped quickly to the living room window and peeked out. A police cruiser sat parked on the street in front of his house.

Relief flooded over Jeffrey's face. At least he was safe, but he knew something bad must have happened to Pablo. With his heart thumping hard in his chest, he hurried to the front door.

"Open up!" the voice called.

"I'm coming," Jeffrey said.

He unlocked the front door and swung it open. Wolfe and Ratburn stood outside. Behind them were Thomas Chan and the boy in the red headband.

Confusion clouded Jeffrey's face.

Wolfe grinned.

"Surprise!"

Chapter Twenty

Pablo's lip was swollen and spotted with dried blood. A fast-swelling bruise covered his left cheek.

"I'm sorry, Jeffrey," he said, fighting back tears.

He sat sprawled on the floor in the back of a speeding van. Marisol sat next to him, her arm around his shoulders. Susie sat next to them, her knees drawn up under her chin, staring silently at the floor. A wall separated them from whoever was driving the van and black duct tape covered a solitary window on the back door. Jeffrey sat on the floor across from his three friends and blinked in the darkness.

"I tried to send you a message," Pablo said, his body shaking, "but those two cops worked me over."

Jeffery winced. The image of Pablo being punched and beaten by the two men flooded his mind and he felt sick to his stomach.

"I got the message," he said.

Marisol pulled Pablo's trembling body tighter against hers. Her face was streaked with black smudges from the tears she'd cried earlier.

"They hit him hard," she told Jeffrey. "I screamed at them to stop, but they kept hitting him. He wasn't going to tell them anything even when they threatened to kill him, but then they said they were going to kill me."

"I'm sorry, Jeffrey," Pablo said again.

"You don't have to apologize," Jeffrey said. "I'm the one who needs to apologize. This whole thing is my fault."

"It's not your fault, Jeffrey," Marisol said.

"It *is* my fault. I should have known those cops were crooked the first time we met them. The way they blew us off; no honest cop would do that. How could I be so stupid?"

"Don't blame yourself," Marisol said.

"And then when we went to see them a second time," Jeffrey said, his voice bubbling with frustration. "I told them everything we know."

"I was there too," Pablo said. "Blame me."

"Stop it, you guys," Marisol said. "We're all in this together."

Jeffrey looked at Susie. "You okay?"

Susie kept her eyes glued to the floor.

"She's okay," Marisol said. "I think."

"Where's your phone, Susie?" Jeffrey asked.

"They took it," Marisol said. "They tricked us one-by-one into leaving our houses and then those two cops arrested us."

"They didn't arrest us, they kidnapped us," Pablo said. "I wish Eddie Lee had been there. He would have killed those guys."

"Eddie Lee is dead," Jeffrey said quietly. He saw the look of shock on Pablo's face and told him about the call from Father Pat.

"Who do you think did it?" Pablo asked.

"I know who did it. It was the one-eyed man. He got Eddie in the back with that switchblade he carries. I'm sure Eddie never saw it coming."

"That girl Clarisse led us all into a trap," Marisol said.

"She's evil," Susie said, looking up and speaking for the first time.

Jeffrey didn't respond. He thought about Clarisse and felt a mixture of anger and betrayal. He thought of Eddie Lee and tears filled the corners of his eyes. "My dad was right, Pablo. He said I would get someone killed and he was right."

Pablo and Marisol watched him.

Jeffrey sniffled and wiped his nose. "No matter what I do, I end up hurting people. My parents ... you guys ... Eddie Lee ... everyone. I try to do the right thing and it backfires every time. I don't know what's wrong with me." He punched the floor of the van.

"Nothing's wrong with you, Jeffrey," said Marisol. She wanted to say more, but the words wouldn't come. Fresh tears came to her eyes and she lowered her head.

Minutes passed in silence, save for the hum of the van's tires as it hurtled over pavement.

"Where are they taking us?" Susie finally asked.

Jeffrey climbed to his feet. Swaying with the movement of the van, he stepped carefully to the rear door. He scratched at the corner of the black tape covering the window and peeled it up enough to peek out. "We're on the freeway. That's all I can see."

"Should we bust out that window or the door?" Pablo said.

"Not at this speed. We wouldn't survive the jump." Jeffrey stepped back from the door and slid down to a seated position across from his friends.

Marisol shook her head. "We're in a mess."

"Maybe," Jeffrey said. "But at least now we'll find out what this whole operation is about."

"Is that all you care about?" Susie snapped. "What if they kill us? We won't find out anything then."

Jeffrey looked at her. "I'm sorry I got you into this, Susie."

"You didn't get her into this," Marisol said. "I did."

"Let's not start that again," said Pablo.

"Well," Jeffrey said, "there's one good thing about our situation."

"What's that?" Marisol asked.

"If they wanted to kill us, we'd already be dead."

An hour passed. And then another. Pablo lay on his side, curled up in a fetal position with his head in Marisol's lap. The beating from the two police detectives had taken a lot out of him and he slept heavily. Marisol had smoothed Pablo's hair back until he fell asleep, and then she, too, dozed off. Susie slept also, sprawled out on the floor. Jeffrey was wide awake. He guessed the time to be late afternoon or early evening.

The speed of the van seemed to slow down. Jeffrey felt the vehicle make a turn and then speed up again. An hour later, the speed slowed again and the van made another turn, and then another. Jeffrey's friends stirred from their sleep.

"Where are we?" Pablo mumbled.

Jeffrey rose. The road underneath the van was bumpy and he stumbled his way to the window. He lifted the black tape and peered outside. "We're in the desert somewhere." He spotted a Latino man with a weathered face and a wide sombrero hat atop his head, leading a pack of mules across a rural road. "It's just like Los Angeles," Jeffrey said, "more jackasses than people."

He went back to his friends.

Twenty minutes later, the van slowed, turned and ground to a stop. The four friends waited, wide-eyed and fully alert. They heard the driver and passenger side doors open and close, followed by footsteps, and then the squeak of the back door as it swung open. Jeffrey and his friends blinked at the sudden intrusion of light. Thomas and the boy with the red headband stood outside, each holding a gun.

Thomas waved with his gun hand. "Out."

Jeffrey scrambled out of the van and stepped onto the desert earth. His legs felt rubbery after the long trip. The others followed him out of the van, blinking and stretching their legs. The sun was setting fast on the horizon. A large two-story French-styled house stood back thirty yards from the road. Young Chinese men in their late teens and early twenties, holding automatic weapons, patrolled outside the house.

Thomas gestured at the house. "Inside."

Jeffrey and his friends trudged towards the house. Thomas and the boy with the red headband followed behind them.

Pablo grimaced with every step. "Now I know how you felt, Jeffrey," he said. Marisol reached out to help him. "I'm okay," he whispered. As they neared the house, Pablo surveyed the layout of the grounds and the guards that surrounded it. "It's like a military compound," he whispered to Jeffrey. "And look," he nodded to a runway behind the house with a plane waiting. "They even have an air force."

Jeffrey saw the plane and nodded. As they stepped closer to the house, his ears perked up. A mechanical hum, the sound of machinery grew louder with every step.

"Jeffrey," Pablo whispered. "Check it out."

Jeffrey followed Pablo's gaze to the side of the house where a group of armed black teens, dressed in gang attire, shook hands and exchanged cigarettes with some of the Chinese youths patrolling the house.

"It doesn't look like a gang war," Pablo whispered. "It looks more like a negotiation."

They reached the front door of the house and stopped. The boy with the headband stepped around them and opened the front door. The sound of machinery grew instantly louder.

The boy gestured with his gun hand to the open doorway. Jeffrey and his friends stepped into the house. The mechanical sound was deafening and seemed to be coming from the basement below them. Jeffrey and Pablo exchanged a look.

The boy with the headband disappeared down a short hall. Thomas led Jeffrey and his friends up a stairway to the second floor and down a long carpeted hall. The mechanical sound diminished with every step. Thomas stopped at the doorway to a bedroom at the end of the hall and ushered Pablo, Marisol and Susie into the room. As Jeffrey started to follow them, Thomas caught him by the arm. "Not you."

Pablo stepped forward. "We'll go with Jeffrey."

"You'll stay here." Thomas slammed the door closed in Pablo's face.

Inside the bedroom, Pablo tried the knob. "Locked," he said.

Marisol turned to a side door and opened it. "Bathroom."

Susie went to the window and pulled back the drapes. Outside the glass were iron bars. "We're prisoners."

Thomas escorted Jeffrey back down the hall. The mechanical sound grew louder.

Jeffrey wondered why he was being singled out and his hands began to tremble. "What about my friends?" he asked.

"Don't worry about them."

They descended the stairs back to the first floor of the house, walked down another hallway and entered a kitchen. Thomas opened a door, filling the room with the sound of heavy pressing machinery from the basement. Beyond the door was a basement stairway. Thomas gestured with his gun to the stairway. "Down you go."

Jeffrey gripped the wooden bannister and started down the stairs. Behind him, he heard the door slam closed and lock. Ahead of him, the rhythmic hum of machinery grew louder with every step he took. He reached the tile floor of the basement and stopped. Overhead fluorescent lights bathed the room with artificial brightness. A bank of four-color Heidelberg offset printers lined the far wall, humming with life and spewing out sheets of light green paper.

The boy with the red headband sat before an embossing press, working a hand lever. The one-eyed man stood back, observing the machines. He saw Jeffrey, smiled wide and shouted above the din. "Welcome, my friend."

The man beckoned with his hand and Jeffrey stepped forward. "Observe," the man said. He reached into the output tray of the nearest printer and removed a double-sided sheet of light green paper. Smiling, he handed the paper to Jeffrey.

The sheet in Jeffrey's hand was fifteen inches long and thirteen inches wide and contained two columns of twenty-dollar bills, each bearing the face of Andrew Jackson. "Is this real?" Jeffrey asked.

The one-eyed man roared with laughter. "What do you think?"

"It looks real to me, but these bills are missing serial numbers and I don't see the colored watermarks."

"You are very observant, my friend." The man gestured to an industrial paper cutter. "We cut the bills here." He stepped towards the embossing press where the boy with the red headband sat. "And we remove the stiffness here." He picked up a bill that had been run through the embossing press and handed it to Jeffrey. "Observe the texture."

Jeffrey rubbed the bill between his thumb and index finger. The paper felt identical to that of the currency in his own pocket. "It feels real."

"Indeed. That paper you hold is a special blend of cotton and linen. Only one company in the entire world – a paper mill in Switzerland - was willing to sell it to me. I told them I needed the paper to print counterfeit-proof bonds." He chuckled and added, "That paper alone cost me half-a-million dollars. These machines," he waved his arm at the bank of printers, pressers and cutting machines, "another half-a-million dollars. You are looking at a million dollar investment, my friend. Come." He led Jeffrey to an inkjet printer, churning out bills one after the other.

"We apply the iridescent foil by hand. The serial numbers are generated with invoicing software from China and then printed on this machine using a gel ink." The man removed a bill from the output tray of the inkjet printer. With a sly smile on his face, he handed the bill to Jeffrey.

Jeffrey studied the bill carefully. Everything about it, from the feel of the rag paper to the signature of the Secretary of the Treasury looked real.

The one-eyed man reached in his pocket, extracted a twenty-dollar bill and handed it to Jeffrey. Jeffrey held the two bills next to each other and compared every detail, front and back. He could see no difference.

The one-eyed man leaned in close and pointed with his pinky finger at the counterfeit bill. "Observe the tiny security strip."

Jeffrey turned the bill lengthwise, held it up to the light, and read in near microscopic print the words USA TWENTY.

The man said, "I had the paper company in Switzerland add chemicals to the process. That bill will hold up to any type of security pen or black-light test."

"It's a work of art," Jeffrey said.

"Precisely, and that is the finest compliment you can offer. I consider myself an artist of the highest caliber."

Jeffrey laid his hand against the side of the inkjet printer. The machine was burning hot to the touch and he jerked his hand back.

"The printers are working overtime," the man said. "We've been busy the last two months."

"Two months?"

"This is a delicate operation, my friend. An exact science. I told you I am an artist." The man observed the printers before him. "It's also a very large operation."

"How large?"

The one-eyed man turned to Jeffrey and studied him for a long moment.

"Two billion dollars."

"*Two billion dollars?*" Jeffrey stared back in disbelief. "You're printing two billion dollars in counterfeit money?"

"That is what I said, and now you understand why you and your friends are here. I cannot afford anything to stand in the way of my enterprise."

Jeffrey did a quick calculation in his head. "With two billion dollars, you could spend over five million dollars a day for an entire year, or half-a-million dollars every day for more than ten years."

"Your numbers are correct."

"But what can you possibly buy with all that cash? If you try to buy a house with cash, the seller is going to be suspicious. The same with a car or a boat or anything expensive. What good is two billion dollars if you can't spend it?"

"Who said anything about spending it?"

Jeffrey blinked. "I don't understand."

The man shrugged without expression.

"But you have to spend it?" Jeffrey insisted.

"Do I?"

"Otherwise, what's the point?"

"Think. You're supposed to be smart."

"Somebody has to spend this money," Jeffrey said.

The man nodded. "Go on."

"Unless you intend to swap it out for real currency, like at a bank or something."

"And how would I do that? No bank in the world carries two billion dollars in currency."

Jeffrey shook his head. "I don't know."

"Go back to your original premise," the man said.

"If you're not going to trade it for real currency, then somebody has to spend it. I mean, that's the only logical alternative.

And if you're not the one spending it, then you must be planning to sell it to somebody else so they can spend it."

"Now you're using your intellect."

"But whoever buys it is going to be in the same boat as you. How can they possibly spend all that money in cash without arousing suspicion?"

"Unless what?"

"Unless ... unless you have multiple buyers?"

"Precisely."

"But you're talking about hundreds or even thousands of people buying your counterfeit currency. Something like that is going to be impossible to keep secret. Someone is going to get caught and tell the police everything. Someone is going to rat you out. And how long will it take you to find thousands of people to buy your currency? You're talking months, possibly years."

"I'm talking about Sunday night."

Jeffrey furrowed his brow. "I still don't get it."

"Think," the one-eyed man commanded. "Clarisse tells me you're smart. Everything I've read about you tells me you're smart. Surely, you can solve the mystery I'm proposing."

"The guards we saw outside, holding guns," Jeffrey said, "they weren't all Chinese."

The man nodded.

"They looked like gang members," Jeffrey said.

The man nodded again.

Jeffrey's eyes suddenly opened wide. "You're selling two billion dollars in counterfeit currency to the street gangs of Los Angeles!"

The man's crooked grin told Jeffrey he was right. "Not just Los Angeles," the man said, "but all across the country."

"And Sunday is two days before Christmas," Jeffrey said.

"And on the following morning," the man announced proudly, "one day before Christmas, two billion dollars in counterfeit currency will descend upon the retail establishments of your city. Thousands of happy shoppers engaged in a spending spree and the sales clerks only too happy to serve them. By noon, the money will all be spent. The gangs will get what they want: cars, guns, ammunition, drugs, alcohol, clothes, jewelry, and women. And I will get what I want: six hundred million dollars in real American currency to exchange in a foreign bank."

"Mr. Chan, it's brilliant!" Jeffrey gushed.

The one-eyed man bowed in appreciation of the compliment. "You saw the plane in back?"

Jeffrey nodded.

"Late Sunday night," the one-eyed man said, "when my business here is concluded, I will be on that plane, flying to a new country." He motioned for Jeffrey to follow him up the stairs. The mechanical hum of the printers followed them up the stairs.

At the top of the steps, the man unlocked the door and led Jeffrey through the kitchen to a dining room. As they entered the room, the man closed the door behind them and the sound of the basement printers immediately stopped. The sudden quiet was startling. Jeffrey guessed the room to be soundproof.

An immaculate white linen tablecloth covered a table in the center of the room. A chandelier hung from the ceiling and a pair of candles stood waiting in the center of the table.

The one-eyed man went to the head of the table and motioned to the chair opposite him. "Sit."

Jeffrey hesitated.

The man took his seat, picked up a tiny bell and rang it twice. "Sit," he said to Jeffrey. "We'll talk before we eat."

"What about my friends?"

"What about them?"

"They're in a room upstairs. They haven't eaten in hours."

The man shrugged.

"I can't eat while they go hungry."

"Don't worry about them. They will be fed. Now sit."

Jeffrey pulled a heavy wooden chair back from the table and sat down. A side door opened and a limping Chinese servant, dressed in a tight white waiter's jacket, entered the room. The one-eyed man communicated with the servant in sign language. The servant watched, his face stoic and unyielding, and then limped out of the room.

The man studied Jeffrey with his yellow-tinged eye. "Clarisse tells me you are a student of human nature."

"Is she here?"

"Answer the question."

Jeffrey nodded. "Yes, that's true."

'She also tells me you have little respect for the intelligence of your fellow man."

"That's true, too."

The one-eyed man nodded graciously. "We have a lot in common."

"Not really," Jeffrey said. "I believe people are stupid, that's true, but I also believe in man's potential, and the redemption of God. I want to help people. You want to steal from them."

"Very well put, my young friend, but I've lived a lot longer than you, and I am also a student of human nature. You speak of redemption and man's potential. I speak of man's reality. Man will not rise up, as you say. Man will go down in humiliating defeat, leaving only his dead carcass for the worms to feed on. For man is a vile and disgusting creature, no better than an animal."

The door opened and the servant limped into the room carrying a bottle of champagne and two glasses.

The one-eyed man flashed a thin smile at Jeffrey. "You can speak freely in front of him," he said, indicating the servant. "He was born deaf and I had his tongue removed years ago so he is unable to talk."

Jeffrey's eyes widened. He glanced at the servant, but the man gave no indication that he heard anything. Jeffrey watched as the servant set the champagne bottle on the table and placed a glass before both he and the one-eyed man. Taking a lighter from his pocket, the servant lit the candles on the table. He limped to the light switch on the wall, turned it low, and left the room. The candlelight cast the room in an eerie glow.

As soon as the door closed behind the servant, Jeffrey leaned across the table and whispered harshly, "How could you do that? How could you be so cruel?"

"I do not look at my actions as cruel. I see them as efficient tasks necessary to my work. Which brings me to you, my friend. That man whose body you found and took to the hospital, Kevin Wong. You sought to solve his murder, but for what purpose?"

"Justice."

"And what is justice?"

"It's doing the right thing."

"Right and wrong, justice and injustice, these are relative terms."

"They're not relative at all. Right is right, and wrong is wrong."

"By whose standards?"

"God's."

The one-eyed man laughed scornfully. "God? Don't talk to me about God. I am a realist."

"So am I."

"Did it ever occur to you that some people deserve to die?"

"People who commit murder deserve to die," Jeffrey said, "but not innocent people."

"Death is the natural order of life. You said yourself that people are stupid, so why should they be allowed to live?"

"I agree with you that people are stupid, but that doesn't mean they should die. God doesn't judge people by how smart they are."

"Perhaps your God does not, but I do. Kevin Wong was stupid. He stole currency from me from a test batch, not nearly as authentic as the bills I showed you. He was spending that inferior currency. If I had allowed him to continue, those inferior bills would have been detected and it would have jeopardized my entire operation. His death was rather unfortunate, but it was necessary. Should I have allowed someone that stupid to live?"

Before Jeffrey could respond, the man said, "In China, intelligence is valued highly. In your country, not so much. Chinese people consider Americans to be among the stupidest people in all the world."

"I can't argue with that."

"You are familiar with my son, Thomas?"

Jeffrey nodded.

The man frowned. "He is my son, and yet I am profoundly disappointed in him, particularly his intellect. It comes from his mother, not from me. To put it kindly, he is an ignoramus. Yes, he is useful for some of the cruder aspects of this business, but his brain is incapable of grasping the larger complexities. He never should have left that body in the yard where you found it. If not for that, you wouldn't be here. But perhaps it was meant to be. Perhaps you are the silver lining to the cloud Thomas created."

"What cloud?" Jeffrey said. "I don't understand."

The one-eyed man reached for the champagne bottle. He uncorked the bottle and poured himself a glass. Then he rose, strode to Jeffrey's end of the table and filled Jeffrey's glass. Jeffrey stared at the fizzing bubbles.

The man took his seat back at the head of the table. His solitary eye studied Jeffrey. "I need a protégée, someone of superior intelligence to carry on my work." He waved a lazy finger in Jeffrey's direction. "I could use you."

"*Me?*"

The man laughed and fondled his champagne glass. "I recognize a superior mind when I see it. You just need the right push. You have the necessary intelligence, the necessary degree of cunning. I can teach you the rest."

"But you don't know anything about me."

"I know everything about you. I know that you possess intelligence far greater than the average man, far greater even than my own. Along with this intelligence, you have a morbid fascination with the criminal mind. Your search for the truth is the driving force of your life. Your need to unlock what remains hidden, to solve the unsolvable, can at times be greater than your own will to live. Am I correct?"

"Maybe."

The man scoffed. "Of course, I am correct."

"How do you know all this?" Jeffrey asked quietly.

"I have my methods. Consider my offer. All the money you want. All the women you want. Whatever you wish, it can all be yours."

"I can't agree to that."

"If you value your life, you will accept my offer."

"What about my friends?"

"They will be dealt with."

"What do you mean 'dealt with'?"

"I mean they will be handled in the most appropriate way."

"You mean you're going to kill them," Jeffrey said.

The man shrugged.

"How can you kill them?" Jeffrey said, his voice rising. "They're young, and they shouldn't even be here. This whole thing is my fault."

"They are witnesses to my work."

"But you'll be gone. You said yourself that you'll be flying out of here late Sunday night."

"In my profession there is always the unexpected."

Jeffrey stared back across the table. *Always the unexpected.* His father had uttered those very same words.

"I cannot afford to take any risks," the man said. "Except with you. I am offering you an opportunity to save your own life and become rich in the process." He grinned slyly. "Do you find Clarisse pretty?"

Jeffrey felt his face blushing red.

"She can be yours," the man said. "Along with everything else you could possibly want for the rest of your life."

"But it's not that easy," Jeffrey protested. "You're about to make six hundred million dollars, but it's not enough. In a few months or a few years, you'll be plotting another crime."

"The challenge invigorates me. The rewards are immeasurable."

"What good are your rewards if you end up in hell?"

The one-eyed man laughed loudly. "Hell? What is hell?"

"You know what hell is."

"It is a figment of your own mind. I do not believe in hell."

"You'll believe it when you get there."

The man's smile vanished and he leaned back in his chair. "I could kill you for saying that. The only reason you are still alive now is Clarisse. Like a child who befriends the family hog before it is slaughtered, she has become fond of you and your companions."

"So you are planning to kill us?"

"All except you."

"If I say 'yes' to your offer, will you let the others go?"

The man slapped the table with the flat of his hand. "Do you take me for a fool?"

"No sir. I'm just asking."

"To follow me, you must be ruthless. So let this be your first test. You live, your friends die."

Jeffrey started to protest, but the man put up his hands, stopping him. "Think carefully of what I'm proposing," he said. "I will tell you more in the morning."

He looked into Jeffrey's eyes and raised his champagne glass. "To crime," he said, and his yellow-tinged eye glowed in the candlelight.

Chapter Twenty-One

"Stale rice and warm water," Pablo said. "That's what they fed us."

"We saved some for you, Jeffrey," Marisol added, a hopeful tilt to her voice.

"We're just glad you're back with us," said Susie. "We were worried about you."

"Thanks," Jeffrey said. He was back in the upstairs bedroom with his friends. They sat cross-legged on the hardwood floor. Outside the window, stars sprinkled across the night sky. The sound of the printers coming from the basement was a distant whir.

Jeffrey told them about the printing operation and the counterfeit money, but not about his dinner conversation with the one-eyed man.

"You were right, Jeffrey," said Pablo. "All along you were right."

"The plan is to sell the counterfeit money to the street gangs on Sunday night," Jeffrey explained, "and then take off in the plane. They're going to some foreign country. They didn't tell me which one."

"What about us?" Susie asked.

Jeffrey sighed. "That I don't know."

"Sunday is the day after tomorrow," Susie said.

"Maybe they'll let us go," Jeffrey said, "and maybe they won't."

Pablo and the girls tensed and exchanged looks.

"What about Clarisse?" asked Marisol. "Remember, when we were at the bowling alley, Thomas told her she had to be here on Sunday night."

Jeffrey shook his head. "I haven't seen her."

"She double-crossed us," said Susie.

"That's one way of looking at it," Jeffrey said. "Then again, she might be the only reason we're still alive."

Jeffrey lay on the floor in the dark and stared up at the ceiling. The window was cracked open and a desert breeze played against the drapes, sending shadows across the ceiling above. Jeffrey watched the shadows and waited until he was sure he heard the rhythmic breathing of deep sleep coming from Marisol and Susie on the bed. Then he rolled onto his side and nudged Pablo, sleeping on the floor next to him.

Pablo stirred and checked his watch. "It's one o'clock," he muttered.

"I had to wait until the girls were asleep," Jeffrey whispered. "I don't want them to hear this."

Pablo nodded, wide awake now.

"We have to think fast," Jeffrey whispered. "We need an escape plan. Can you come up with something?"

"I can try," Pablo whispered back, "only we don't have any have weapons. We don't have anything. Even if we're able to slip out of here, how are we going to survive out in the desert with no water and no food? We wouldn't last two days."

"Maybe we can hoard some tomorrow."

"Sure, we can try. I'd rather take my chances out there than in here. There's something else, Jeffrey. We might have to take out a couple of those guards."

"What do you mean 'take out'?"

"You know what I mean. It won't be a sin. They're holding us here against our will. If anything, it would be self-defense."

Jeffrey nodded.

"We have to think about the girls, too," Pablo said. "If we try to escape, they could get hurt or killed. So could we."

"That's a chance we'll have to take," Jeffrey said. "I think our days here are numbered."

Chapter Twenty-Two – 3 Days Before Christmas

"I trust you slept well," said the one-eyed man as he and Jeffrey walked down the hall on the second floor of the villa.

"I slept on the floor," Jeffrey said, "in the same clothes I'm wearing now, wondering if today was going to be my last day on earth."

The man chuckled. "Perhaps what I'm about to show you will lift your spirits."

He led Jeffrey into a bedroom. A king-sized bed occupied the center of the room. On the far wall, a large window led to a balcony that overlooked the rear of the estate. Jeffrey could see the plane, waiting on a makeshift runway, a hundred yards back from the house.

On the side wall of the room, a curtain was pulled back, revealing a large steel vault. The vault door was open and looked to be over a foot thick.

The one-eyed man took Jeffrey by the arm and escorted him to the front of the vault door. He pointed to the combination lock. "Observe, a six-letter combination known only to myself."

The man stepped around the door and into the open vault.

Jeffrey followed him inside.

The vault was constructed of solid steel, ten feet wide by twelve feet long and six feet high. Shelves lined the walls and were piled high with bundles of counterfeit currency. Inside the vault were a small desk and a pair of stools, occupied by Wolfe and Ratburn. The two detectives each used a counting machine to sort the fake currency into packets of one hundred bills, each bundle representing $2,000.

Ratburn glanced over his shoulder. He saw Jeffrey and leapt off his stool. "What's *he* doing here?"

"What's the matter?" Wolfe said. "You nervous?"

"Of course, I'm nervous. Those kids make me nervous." He jerked his thumb back at Jeffrey. "Especially that fat one. Why are they still alive?"

"Relax," said Wolfe.

"Don't tell me to relax. Until we're sitting on a foreign beach, with drinks in our hands and six hundred million in cash, I'm not relaxing." He turned to the one-eyed man. "Why don't you let me do it? I'll finish those kids off real quick."

"In due time," the one-eyed man replied.

Ratburn sat back on his stool and resumed counting. Jeffrey took a couple of steps deeper into the vault. Ratburn turned his head sideways, following Jeffrey from the corner of his eye. "Don't stand behind me, kid. I'll give you a roundhouse kick to the head."

The one-eyed man took Jeffrey by the arm and pulled him away from Ratburn. He pointed to the walls of the vault. "Solid steel, two feet thick. Storm proof. Fireproof. Burglar proof."

"Burglar proof?" Jeffrey said.

The man nodded. "The vault is equipped with a safety mechanism." He pointed to three corners on the ceiling. "Observe three vents. If the vault is breached in any way, without my entering the combination, it will be flooded with poison gas." He chuckled. "If anyone were to break in, they would meet a most excruciating death."

"I'd like to see that," Ratburn said.

"How would you get the money then?" Jeffrey asked. "Wouldn't the poison make it untouchable?"

"On the contrary," the man said. He pointed to a fourth corner on the ceiling, to the right of the vault door. "Here we have the antidote: a chemical solution to clear the gas. Its only drawback is time. It takes twenty-four hours to clear the vault of gas. By that time, the corpse of the dead will be rotting."

Jeffrey frowned.

The one-eyed man turned to Wolfe: "May I see you for a moment? About what we discussed earlier."

Wolfe nodded and rose from his stool. He glanced guiltily at Ratburn and then followed the one-eyed man and Jeffrey out of the vault.

"Don't take too long," Ratburn called after them. "We've got a lot of counting to do."

Outside the vault, the one-eyed man gave a small nod and Wolfe swung the heavy vault door shut. The one-eyed man beckoned Jeffrey with his finger. Jeffrey followed the man to a control panel with a microphone, a timer, and three black-and-white video monitors. Each of the monitors displayed a different angle of the interior of the vault. Below the monitors was a row of buttons and switches.

Jeffrey watched on the monitors as Ratburn tried to open the vault door from the inside.

"Observe the timer and lock," the one-eyed man told Jeffrey, and he set the timer for thirty seconds. He fished a key out of his pocket, locked the timer in place with the key, and returned the key to his pocket.

"What are you doing?" Jeffrey asked.

"You shall see." The man pressed a button on the control panel and spoke into the microphone. "Can you hear me?"

On the video monitors, Jeffrey saw Ratburn react to the man's question.

"Press the red intercom button," the one-eyed man said.

Jeffrey watched as Ratburn pressed a button on the wall by the vault door.

"I can hear you," came Ratburn's voice. "What's going on?"

"I want to thank you for your service," said the one-eyed man. "You have been a tremendous help to my organization." He nudged Jeffrey and pointed to the timer, which read fifteen seconds and counting.

"Quit fooling around and open the door," Ratburn said. "I told you before I get claustrophobic."

The man pressed the intercom button. "I have the cure for your claustrophobia." He took his finger off the button and said to Jeffrey, "This is what we call 'one less mouth to feed'."

"What are you talking about?" said Ratburn.

Jeffrey watched wide-eyed as the timer reached zero. He heard three successive clicks and watched on the monitor screens as the three vents in the ceiling corners of the vault rolled back and began spewing clouds of poison gas into the vault.

Ratburn reacted instantly, his body twisting and contorting, screaming in silence.

"You're killing him," Jeffrey shouted. He lunged for the control panel, frantically flipping switches and pushing buttons to try and stop the gassing.

Wolfe moved in swiftly. He swung a heavy fist into Jeffrey's stomach. Jeffrey doubled over, gasping for air, vomit oozing out of the corners of his mouth. Wolfe raised his arm and chopped the flat of his hand across the back of Jeffrey's neck. Jeffrey collapsed on the floor.

Chapter Twenty-Three

Even before he opened his eyes, Jeffrey could feel the sharp, biting throb across the back of his neck. When his eyes did open, Clarisse's young face was over his, lined with concern, and framed by soft, dark hair. She laid a delicate hand on his forehead and smoothed back his hair.

"What happened?" Jeffrey mumbled.

"Wolfe beat you up," she said simply.

He started to draw his knees up and felt a throbbing in the pit of his stomach. His face tensed and he groaned.

"Shhh," she whispered. "Lie still. I will take care of you."

Without his glasses, the room was blurry, but Jeffrey could see that he was stretched out on a bed. Clarisse was in a chair by the side of the bed. The room was quiet and had no windows. He didn't know if it was night or day.

Clarisse reached into a plastic pan on the nightstand by the bed and removed a small dripping towel. Jeffrey closed his eyes. He heard the gentle dribble of water as Clarisse wrung the towel out over the pan. Seconds later, he felt the warm, damp towel across his forehead. A bead of warm water rolled down to the corner of his eye and then down the side of his face.

"Where are my glasses?" he said, his eyes still closed.

"I have them."

"I can't see without them."

"I will give them to you when I decide. Right now, just rest."

"How long have I been here?"

"Three hours."

"How long have you been here?"

He waited for a response. Her silence told him that she had been at his side the entire time.

"Clarisse?"

"Shhh! I told you – rest."

He opened his eyes. Her eyes, dark and beautiful, were on his. "Where are my friends?" he asked.

"Your friends are being taken care of."

"Do you know what happened?"

"About what?"

"They killed a man. Your uncle and Wolfe. They gassed him to death in the vault." He waited, but again she did not respond. She removed the towel from his forehead and rinsed it in the pan. "Did you hear me?" he asked.

"I heard what happened." She paused a moment and added, "I told you before, he's not my uncle." She wrung the towel out over the pan and placed it fresh on his forehead.

As her hands pulled away, Jeffrey reached for them. He caught her nearest hand and she accepted, clasping his hand tight against hers. Her fingers felt warm and wet against his. She smiled down on him. It was the first time he had seen her smile.

"Are you going to tell me what's going on?" he said. He felt her hand attempt to pull away, but he held fast.

She lowered her eyes. "I cannot tell you everything."

"Why not?"

"It would not be good."

"For who?"

She lifted her eyes. "For both of us."

"Your uncle – or whoever that guy is – he wants me to join him. He wants me to be his assistant or something."

"And you accepted?" Her voice was hopeful.

Jeffrey pulled his hand away. "No, I can't do that."

"Why not?"

"Why do you think? First, he's planning on killing my friends. Second, I'd be committing a mortal sin and condemning my soul to hell."

"We could be friends," she said. Her voice broke and she had the same lonely look that Jeffrey first saw in her at the house in Monterey Park.

"No offense," he said quietly, "but no friendship is worth going to hell for."

She pushed her chair back from the bed. Jeffrey could sense a wall coming between them.

"You have to get us out of here, Clarisse."

"There's nothing I can do."

"There *is* something you can do. Call the police and tell them what's going on here."

Clarisse shook her head. "That would not solve anything. It would lead to a shootout and we'd all be killed."

"Then you have to sneak us out."

"You wouldn't last more than a day in the desert and if you took the road, they would find you and kill you."

"So you're going to let us all die?"

Clarisse rose suddenly to her feet. Her chair toppled back and thudded softly on the carpeted floor. "I'm trying to help you," she said, tears coming to her eyes. "I don't want to see you die."

"I'm trying to help *you*," Jeffrey said. "Look, I don't want to die, either. But my soul is clean and I believe in the true Catholic faith. If I die, I'm going to Heaven. But you – you're an accessory to murder and who knows what else. If you die, your soul is going straight to hell for all eternity."

"Don't say that," she pleaded.

"It's true. Whether you believe it or not, it's true."

"I studied those things you told me about: Fatima and the image of Guadalupe. Some people say they're fake."

"Some people are idiots. But they can't dispute the evidence without making up lies."

"You say Heaven is a place of beauty and happiness. But what if my parents are not there? If I do what you say and I go to Heaven, how can I be happy if my parents are not there?"

Jeffrey frowned. "That's an excellent question. You'll have to ask God that one yourself. I don't know the answer."

"I thought you knew everything."

Jeffrey chuckled. "I don't know everything. I wish I did."

"Do you ever think you could be wrong? About God and going to Heaven?"

Jeffrey thought for a long moment. "Sometimes," he said. "But then I look at the evidence and it convinces me that I'm right."

"How do I go to Heaven?"

"First, you have to embrace the true Catholic faith, not what passes for the Catholic faith today. What passes for the Catholic faith today is a counterfeit religion, as phony as the money you're printing here. You need the true Catholic faith. Then you need to come clean and follow the true Church's teachings. And you need to be baptized."

"Will I go to jail?"

"Maybe. But at your age, maybe not. I'll do everything I can to help you. I promise you that. And then – if you still want – we can be friends."

Clarisse cast her eyes downward. "I have to think about what you are saying."

"There isn't much time."

"I know," she said.

"We could all be dead tomorrow."

"I know," she said.

"You need a doctor," Marisol said, her eyes shifting from Jeffrey to Pablo and back to Jeffrey, "both of you."

It was late at night and Jeffrey was back in the room with his friends, the four of them seated on the floor.

"Fat chance of that happening," Pablo said.

"Did you give any thought to what we talked about?" Jeffrey asked him.

Marisol and Susie sat up straight and eyed both boys.

"What did you guys talk about?" Susie said.

Pablo hesitated.

"Tell us," said Marisol. "We deserve to know."

Pablo glanced at Jeffrey who gave him a small nod. "We talked about an escape plan," Pablo said. "I came up with two possible plans. Plan A is to break the mirror in the bathroom and use the glass to try and cut through the bars on the window. There's also a nail file in there that we can use."

"I saw that," Susie said.

"If we can cut through those bars, we can jump or lower ourselves out the window and make a run for it. The problem is all those armed guards surrounding the place. Plus, if we make it to the desert, we wouldn't last more than a day or two without water. We'd have to guzzle as much water as we could from the bathroom faucet before we left and then make like camels."

"I'm not a good camel," Susie said.

"Plan B," Pablo said, "is to jump one of those guards when they bring us our food and take their phone. We'd have to knock him out or even kill him, but then we'd have his phone and his gun. We can use the phone to call the police. The problem is I don't know where we are or what address to give them."

"The 9-1-1 operator can trace the call to the phone and its location," Marisol said.

"You can call the Secret Service, too, Jeffrey," said Pablo. "You said you had that agent's phone number memorized."

Jeffrey nodded.

"There are two more problems to the plan," Pablo said.

The others looked at him anxiously.

Pablo nodded at Jeffrey. "Between the two of us, I think we could take one of those guards, but you're in no condition to fight right now. The second problem is that even if we do take out one of the guards, we'll likely be stuck up here. Like Plan A, there are too many guards outside to sneak past. So we'll have to hole up here, maybe in this room, until the cops come. If anyone comes after us, we can use the gun to hold them off, but I don't know how much ammunition we'll have and how long we'll be able to hold anyone off."

"That sounds really dangerous," Susie said.

"Staying here is dangerous," said Marisol.

"They're both dangerous," Pablo said, "so we'll have to decide."

Jeffrey lowered his head and withdrew into himself. He thought about Ratburn dying in the vault, his body contorted in pain. Unless there was a way that he could outsmart the one-eyed man, he knew he and friends would likely be dead within forty-eight hours.

"Jeffrey?"

It was Pablo's voice. Jeffrey blinked and looked up. His three friends were all watching him.

"What do you say, Jeffrey?" Pablo asked.

"Let's try the window," Jeffrey said. "We'll try cutting through those bars in the morning."

Chapter Twenty-Four –2 Days Before Christmas

It was not yet dawn when Marisol and Susie awoke to the sound of breaking glass. Both girls sat up in bed before they realized the sound came from the bathroom. Pablo had used his shoe to crack a corner of the bathroom mirror and then pried off a piece of glass.

Pablo used the glass and Jeffrey used the nail file to saw at the bars outside the window. Marisol and Susie listened at the door for the sound of anyone approaching.

By noon, the boys had managed to saw through one of the iron bars. By five o'clock, they'd sawed through a second bar, and by ten o'clock that night, they'd made it through a third bar, enough room for all of them except Jeffrey to fit through. It was then that the cars began arriving.

Jeffrey and Pablo stood watch at the window, counting the cars that parked behind the house, and the occupants that emerged and went into the house. By eleven-thirty, they'd counted over two hundred cars and over four hundred gang members.

Some of the gang members went inside the house, stayed a short while, and then emerged carrying black satchels and drove away. Most of them remained inside and many milled around the back of the house, exchanging handshakes and greetings.

184 / Mike Mains

"This is insane," Pablo said. "It's like every criminal in the country is coming here tonight."

"What about our escape plan?" Susie asked.

"We'll have to wait until they leave," Jeffrey said. "At least some of them. This place is crawling with gang members. We'd never make it out of here."

Loud rap music began to play from the first floor of the house. Ten minutes later, the door flung open and Wolfe stepped into the room, followed by the one-eyed man, both men holding guns.

"Let's go," Wolfe said.

"Go where?" said Jeffrey.

"You'll see."

The one-eyed man led them down the hall to the room with the vault. As Jeffrey, Pablo and Marisol filed into the room, Wolfe grabbed Susie by the arm and pulled her aside.

"What are you doing?" she cried.

"Shut up," Wolfe said, and pulled her roughly down the hall.

Jeffrey, Pablo and Marisol stopped and watched. The one-eyed man stood in the doorway between them and Wolfe and Susie. He held his gun and smiled.

"Let me go," Susie shrieked as Wolfe pulled her further down the hall.

"Come along quietly if you don't want a broken arm," Wolfe told her.

"Where are you taking her?" Marisol demanded.

"That is no concern of yours," said the one-eyed man. He waved his gun at the open vault. "Inside."

"Susie!" Marisol called.

The one-eyed man shoved her towards the vault door.

"Hey!" Pablo yelled, and took a step towards the one-eyed man.

The man leveled his gun at Pablo's chest. "Into the vault. Now."

Pablo backed away and followed Jeffrey and Susie into the vault.

The one-eyed man stopped in the doorway. His yellow-tinged eye focused on Jeffrey with a burning intensity. "I offered you an opportunity to partake in my little enterprise, but you wouldn't listen. Very well. Now you'll have to die." He stepped out of the vault and the heavy steel door swung shut.

"Wait," cried Jeffrey, but it was too late. He heard the combination lock turn. He and his friends were locked inside the airtight vault.

Pablo rushed to the inside of the vault door and grabbed hold of the cold metal handle. The cordlike muscles on his forearms strained as he pushed, pulled, twisted and turned, but it was no use. The door wouldn't budge.

He stopped and stepped back, his face flushed and his chest heaving. "We're trapped," he said. "Trapped like rats."

"At least until somebody finds us," said Marisol. Her eyes shifted from one boy to the other. "I mean, eventually someone will have to find us, won't they?"

Jeffrey slumped against the side of the vault and slid down to a seated position on the concrete floor. "It's worse than that," he said.

"What's worse?" said Marisol.

The image of Ratburn, twisting and contorting his body in the gas-filled vault, flooded Jeffrey's mind and he felt a sick churning in his stomach. He looked up into the hopeful eyes of his young friends, but he didn't have the heart to reveal what was in store for them.

Pablo kneeled down next to him. "What is it, Jeffrey?"

"He said we have to die. That means he set the timer."

"What timer?"

Jeffrey straightened his glasses. "This vault comes with a safety mechanism. It's designed to go off in case of a break-in, but it's also connected to a timer which can be set in the next room. When the safety mechanism is activated, the vault is flooded with poison gas."

Marisol gasped and covered her mouth. Pablo's face glazed white as a sheet. An intercom buzzed and they heard the voice of the one-eyed man coming from a loudspeaker. "Can you hear me, boy? If you can, press the intercom button on the wall."

Jeffrey leapt to his feet and pressed a red button on the wall by the vault door. "I can hear you." Pablo and Marisol crowded in close behind him, shoulders touching. They waited for the man's response.

"I've set the timer for midnight, exactly fifteen minutes from now. That's all the time I need to make my escape. If not, I can use your young lives as leverage. Of course, at this point, I fully intend to get away. I wish I could tell you that the gas is painless, but it's not. It's excruciatingly painful." The man chuckled. "I could describe to you the unspeakable agony you will soon experience, but perhaps it's better if you imagine it for yourselves. No one will save you and no one will hear you scream. Goodbye."

The intercom buzzed and went dead.

Marisol screamed.

Pablo leaned over Jeffrey's shoulder and jammed the red intercom button. "Hey! Hey! Come back!"

Jeffrey took off his glasses and covered his face with his hands. There was no way out. He was going to die and his friends were going to die, and everything was his fault. He felt himself panicking and his mind went blank. How did it happen? How did they get there? He thought back to the fateful morning when he and Pablo found Kevin Wong's body, and images from the last two weeks flashed across his mind.

"Jeffrey! Jeffrey!"

It was Pablo's voice.

Jeffrey blinked and saw his two friends staring at him with horror-stricken faces.

"What do we do?" Pablo said.

Jeffrey slid his glasses back on. "Okay," he said, "the first thing we have to do is look for an alternative way out of here."

"What do you mean?" said Marisol.

"A trap door, an escape door, a hidden panel ... Tap along the walls and floor and listen for a hollow sound. It's a longshot, but we have to try it."

The shelves lining the walls were empty. Jeffrey and his friends went around the room, tapping the floor, tapping the walls between the shelves and along the side of the vault door, hoping and praying for a hollow sound.

Outside the back of the house, Wolfe pulled Susie past the sea of parked cars and towards the waiting plane. The rap music from the house diminished the further they went. They passed half-a-dozen gang members, armed with automatic weapons, and sitting atop the hoods of a pair of cars. The gangsters hooted and whistled at Susie as Wolfe dragged her past.

Footsteps sounded behind them. Wolfe turned to see the one-eyed man jogging to catch up with them.

"Everything is taken care of," the one-eyed man said.

"Too bad about the fat kid, huh?" Wolfe said.

"He had his chance."

They reached a boarding ladder at the front of the plane. Wolfe climbed aboard, dragging Susie with him. The one-eyed man followed.

Clarisse rose from a passenger seat in the cabin and approached them with questioning eyes.

The one-eyed man saw her and smiled. "It's done," he said.

Wolfe shoved Susie past Clarisse towards the passenger seats. "Sit down," he said. Susie took the first seat in the front row of the plane's twenty passenger seats.

Across the aisle from her, Yankee, Doodle, and Dandy peered out of their travel cases. Each dog occupied a separate seat, their cases held in place by a seat belt. The little dogs watched Susie with long faces and big soulful eyes. The seat directly behind Susie was empty and the plane's remaining fifteen passenger seats held satchels stuffed with six hundred million dollars in real currency.

Clarisse watched as Wolfe pulled a pair of handcuffs from his pocket. He cuffed Susie's nearest wrist and locked the other cuff around the seat's armrest.

Clarisse turned to the one-eyed man. "How much time do we have?"

"We're leaving now."

"*Right* now?"

The man checked his watch. "Fifteen minutes."

Clarisse started for the door.

"Where are you going?" the man asked.

"Bathroom."

"We have a bathroom on the plane."

"I don't like using it."

She stepped out the door to the boarding ladder.

The one-eyed man and Wolfe exchanged a look.

Chapter Twenty-Five

Jeffrey and his friends stood helplessly in the middle of the vault. They had tapped along every conceivable inch of the walls, floor and ceiling and found nothing. They looked at each other, none of them knowing what to say, none of them daring to speak the inevitable.

Jeffrey took a sheet of paper and a pen from the desk and sat down on the floor.

"What are you doing?" Pablo asked him.

"Writing my will. If we're going to die, we might as well do it right. I'm going to leave everything I have to Father Pat. He can sell it and use the money to help save souls."

"Put me in there too," said Pablo, and he sat on the floor across from Jeffrey.

"And me," Marisol said. She sat on the floor next to Pablo.

Jeffrey shook the pen a couple of times. He thought for a moment, and then spoke aloud as he wrote. "To Whom It May Concern, as I approach the end of my miserable life, I, Jeffrey Jones, and my friends, Pablo Reyes and Marisol Rodriguez, do hereby bequeath all of our meager possessions to Father Pat, including all my books ..."

"And my old comic book collection from when I was kid," Pablo said.

"And Pablo's old comic book collection," Jeffrey wrote.

"And my doll collection from when I was a little girl," Marisol said.

"And Marisol's doll collection from when she was little," Jeffrey wrote.

"And my pet raccoon," Marisol added.

Jeffrey and Pablo both looked at her. "Pet raccoon?"

"Well, he's not really my pet, but he comes around our backyard and I leave food for him."

"And Marisol's pet raccoon," Jeffrey wrote, "and all the other useless junk that we have accumulated over the years." He stopped suddenly and tore the paper in half.

"What's wrong?" Marisol asked.

Jeffrey flung the two halves of the paper into the air. "This is like giving up. There's got to be a way out of here. There's got to be!"

"But how?" Marisol asked.

"I don't know!" Jeffrey shouted.

"Don't yell at me, Jeffrey."

"I'm not yelling. I'm trying to think!"

"But we *are* going to die."

"Don't say that!"

"But it's true!" Marisol turned to Pablo. "It's true, isn't it, Pablo?"

"Then we should be praying!" Jeffrey said, "Who cares about our junk?"

"I don't want to die," Marisol said.

They heard a buzzing sound from the intercom, followed by a female voice saying, "Hello?"

For a moment, Jeffrey and his friends sat motionless, looking back and forth at each other in startled surprise, then they leapt to their feet.

Jeffrey pushed the intercom button. "Yes! Who is this?"

"It's me, Clarisse."

"Thank God," Marisol gushed.

Jeffrey pressed the button. "Clarisse, do you know the combination to the vault?"

"No, I do not."

"Oh, no," said Marisol.

"Okay," Jeffrey said into the intercom to Clarisse. "Okay. Is there another way out of here?"

"I don't know. I doubt it."

"Is there any way you can open the vault door?"

"Not without the combination."

"There's a timer on the control panel where you are. Can you turn it off?"

Jeffrey and his friends waited. Seconds ticked by. Clarisse's voice said, "I can't. He's locked it."

"Clarisse," Jeffrey said. "We're going to die in here if we don't get this vault open by midnight."

"I know that."

Jeffrey turned to his friends, his forehead glistening with sweat. "We have to solve that combination and we have to do it quickly. It's six letters long."

"How can we possibly do that?" asked Marisol. "There are millions of six letter combinations."

"We'll just have to puzzle it out," Jeffrey said. "Either that or we die."

Pablo checked his watch. "We have four minutes."

"Oh, God," said Marisol, her face turning white.

Jeffrey took a deep breath and pressed the intercom button. "Clarisse, do you have any idea of what the combination might be? Any clues from Mr. Chan at all?"

"No."

"Do you know any of the passwords he uses on any of his accounts or devices?"

"No."

"Most people pick something personal," Marisol said, "so it'll be easier to remember."

Jeffrey spoke to Clarisse: "Do you know when his birthday is?"

"Yes, I know that."

"Okay, try that. Use two digits for the year. That will make it six numbers long."

A moment later, Clarisse responded, "No, that didn't work."

"Where was he born?"

"In Shanghai."

"That's too many letters," Jeffrey said. "Try his son's name. Try Thomas."

A moment later, Clarisse responded, "No, that didn't work."

"Three minutes," said Pablo.

Jeffrey pressed the intercom button. "What's the name of Thomas's mother?"

"Isabel."

"That's six letters," Pablo said.

"Okay," Jeffrey said to Clarisse. "Try Isabel."

Clarisse responded, "No."

Jeffrey turned to his friends. "What are some words that might be significant?"

"Crime," said Pablo, "money, counterfeit, currency."

Jeffrey shook his head. "None of those are six letters."

"Secret Service," Pablo said.

Jeffrey pressed the intercom button. "Clarisse, try the word 'secret' and then try the word 'service'."

"No and no," came the response.

"Andrew Jackson," said Pablo. "His name's on the twenty-dollar bill."

Jeffrey counted the letters of both names quickly on his fingers, and then pressed the intercom button. "Try Andrew."

"No," came the response.

"How much time, Pablo?" Marisol asked.

"Two minutes."

"Think," Jeffrey said. "Think!"

"Wait, I have an idea," Marisol said. "People sometimes name their passwords after their pets."

"Great idea!" Jeffrey said. He pressed the intercom button. "Clarisse, try Yankee."

"No," Clarisse responded, "that didn't work."

"Try Doodle and Dandy."

"Dandy is five letters," said Pablo.

Jeffrey pressed the button. "Spell Dandy, D-A-N-D-E-E."

"None of those worked," Clarisse responded, her voice breaking.

"Famous criminals," said Pablo.

"Like who?" asked Marisol.

"Dillinger, Al Capone, Ma Barker."

Jeffrey spoke to Clarisse, "Try Capone and Barker." He turned to Pablo. "Who else?"

Pablo shrugged. "That's all I know."

Clarisse responded, "No, Jeffrey, they didn't work."

Pablo punched the wall of the vault.

"What do I do, Jeffrey?" Clarisse wailed.

"Stay calm," Jeffrey told her. He turned to his friends, his face and shirt soaked with sweat. "How much time, Pablo?"

"One minute."

Marisol reached for Pablo and hugged him. Pablo hugged her back.

Jeffrey hung his head and slumped against the wall. Pablo glanced his way. "Why does it have to be like this?" he said. "It's just like Father Pat said: Everything is backwards, everything is upside down."

Jeffrey spun around to face him, his eyes wide open. "That's it!"

"What's it?"

"What you just said! Everything is backwards, everything is upside down!" He lunged for the intercom button and shouted, "Clarisse, try Yankee backwards!"

"Backwards?"

"Yes, spell it E-E-K-N-A-Y."

Pablo and Marisol broke off their embrace and crowded in close behind Jeffrey.

"It didn't work," Clarisse said.

"Try Doodle backwards," Jeffrey said. "E-L-D-O-O-D."

"No, Jeffrey," Clarisse wailed, "they're not working."

Jeffrey slammed his fist down on the desktop.

Pablo checked his watch. "Twelve seconds, Jeffrey."

"Quick," Jeffrey said, "what's that actor's name from the movie, *Yankee Doodle Dandy*?"

"My grandmother has that movie," Marisol said. "His name is James Cagney."

Jeffrey jammed the intercom button. "Clarisse, try Cagney." He glanced at Marisol as he spelled the letters. "C-A-G-N-E-Y." Marisol nodded.

"No, Jeffrey!"

"Try Cagney backwards! Y-E-N-G-A-C."

They heard a grating, metallic sound above them and looked up to see the three corner vents opening.

Marisol screamed.

Jeffrey shouted into the intercom, "Hurry, Clarisse!"

Clarisse's voice squealed back, "It worked!"

Jeffrey and Pablo threw their weight against the heavy vault door and shoved it open. Marisol followed them out of the vault and into the bedroom.

From the vault, three clicks sounded, followed by hissing gas. Jeffrey and Pablo hurried to the front of the steel door and swung it closed. The door locked into place.

Jeffrey slumped back against the vault door, drained. Clarisse threw her arms around his neck and hugged him.

Marisol fainted into Pablo's arms.

Chapter Twenty-Six

Loud rap music blared from the house beneath them. The throbbing beat shook the walls and the foundation of the house. Jeffrey felt the floor vibrating under his feet.

"Listen," Clarisse shouted over the din. "Listen very carefully. There isn't much time."

Marisol blinked and fanned her face, regaining consciousness. Pablo steadied her.

"The representatives from every gang in Los Angeles are here," Clarisse explained, "over two hundred of them. They'll be leaving in the morning when the stores open. Until then it's going to be one long party."

A burst of automatic gunfire erupted outside.

Jeffrey, Pablo and Marisol all ducked.

"Don't worry," Clarisse told them. "It's just the gangs showing off. They're shooting at snakes and lizards in the desert. It's their way of having fun."

"They call that fun?" Pablo said.

"You don't have to worry. Nobody is supposed to come upstairs. In the morning, when the gangs have left, you can escape. Until then, keep quiet and hopefully no one will find you up here."

"*Hopefully?*" Marisol said.

"Lock the door behind me," Clarisse said, "and don't open it or let anyone in, not even me."

"Where are you going?" Jeffrey said.

Clarisse checked the time on her phone. "I'm leaving in nine minutes. The plane is waiting." Her eyes met Jeffrey's. "I did what I could. I can't do anymore. Goodbye, Jeffrey."

She turned to leave. Jeffrey grabbed her arm. "Where's Susie?"

Clarisse glanced quickly at Marisol, and at Jeffrey. "She's on the plane. They're taking her with them."

"Taking her where?" Marisol demanded.

"Out of the country."

"Why?"

Clarisse lowered her eyes.

"It's called white slavery," Jeffrey said. "Human trafficking."

Marisol gasped.

Jeffrey turned to Clarisse. "You've got to get us on that plane."

Anxiety flooded the girl's face. "But why?"

"To rescue Susie."

"You can't!"

"We have to. We can't let her die, or ... or worse." He glanced at Marisol. She stared back at him, her lower lip quivering and her face pale.

"You can't possibly rescue her," Clarisse said. "She's hand-cuffed to a seat on the plane, and Wolfe is the only one with a key."

Jeffrey extended his hand. "I need your phone."

Clarisse took a step back. "For what?"

"The first thing we have to do is stop that counterfeit money from hitting the street."

Clarisse hesitated.

"You'll be gone in nine minutes," Jeffrey said. "What do you care if these people here get caught? The police won't catch you."

Clarisse searched his face with her eyes. Reluctantly, she handed him the phone.

"What about Susie?" Marisol said.

Jeffrey held up his hand for quiet. He dialed the number to the Secret Service agent he met ten days ago. White's voice was hoarse as he answered. The call had awoken him.

"This is Jeffrey Jones."

Jeffrey heard shock in the agent's voice. "Jeffrey! You're alive?"

"For now."

"What do you mean 'for now'? Half the city of Los Angeles is looking for you and your friends."

"We're not in Los Angeles," Jeffrey said. He whispered to Clarisse, "What's the address here?" Clarisse told him and he repeated it back to the agent.

"Who's that with you?" White said. "And what's all that noise?"

Jeffrey ignored the questions and said, "There's two billion dollars in counterfeit money at that address I just gave you. In the morning, it's going to flood the streets of Los Angeles."

"Is this a joke?"

Jeffrey gripped the phone tighter. "It's not a joke. And you'd better bring an army, because there are hundreds of armed gang members here."

He heard the agent mutter a profanity.

"Call our parents," Jeffrey told him. "Tell them we love them, and hopefully we'll see them again."

"Now listen, kid," the agent began.

Jeffrey hung up and handed the phone back to Clarisse. "That's one issue fixed. Now about the plane."

"I told you, it's impossible," Clarisse said. She checked the time. "It's leaving in seven minutes."

"You have to get us onboard."

Clarisse's eyes shifted from Jeffrey to Pablo to Marisol, and back to Jeffrey. "They'll kill you. All of you."

"We can't leave Susie."

"Even if it means getting killed yourself?"

"We have to take that chance."

"And then what? Suppose I do get you onboard? How can you possibly rescue your friend? The men have guns."

"I don't know," Jeffrey said, "but we have to try. Once that plane's up in the air, Susie will be gone forever."

He suddenly realized he hadn't consulted his friends about any of this, and he turned to them. He couldn't rescue Susie without Pablo's help, and if he and Pablo were going after Susie, they couldn't leave Marisol here by herself.

Pablo saw the seriousness in Jeffrey's face. He stood up straight and said, "Danger's my middle name, remember?"

"Mine, too," said Marisol. She glanced at Pablo and he glanced back.

"Then it's decided," Jeffrey said. "It's up to you now, Clarisse. It's all up to you."

Clarisse stared back at him. Her eyes were unwavering and her face was like iron.

Chapter Twenty-Seven

Jeffrey's hands trembled as he tore the sheets off the bed. He knew they had to rescue Susie, but how? And if they did make it on the plane, what then? Would they be stuck on an airborne flight with no way out? He needed to think, but the music downstairs made it impossible. The pounding beat was like a jackhammer on his brain.

He tried tying the bed sheets together, but his hands were shaking too hard. Pablo noticed and stepped in. He took the sheets from Jeffrey's hands and tied the ends together. Marisol hurried over with a pair of spare sheets from the closet and they tied them to the others. The four sheets knotted together stretched out twenty feet.

Jeffrey started for the window.

"Wait," Pablo said. He stepped across the room to the light switch by the door and turned it off, plunging the room into darkness. "Okay," he said.

Jeffrey opened the window and Pablo and Marisol followed him out onto the balcony. A cool breeze flowed over them. Stars dotted the sky overhead and the moon was bright, giving them some visibility.

Below them, an overflow of cars spilled out over the desert grounds. Armed gang members, wearing do-rags, wife beaters, and sagging pants, patrolled the area. Sporadic gunfire erupted across the desert. The guards ignored it.

Pablo tapped Jeffrey on the shoulder and pointed out the guards. Jeffrey nodded. Pablo tapped Jeffrey again and pointed to the right. Jeffrey looked and saw the lights and dim outline of the plane idling a hundred yards away. He nodded grimly.

A burst of gunfire echoed in the distance. Bullets hit the picture window behind them, shattering the glass. Jeffrey and his friends dropped to the balcony floor and covered their heads.

Jeffrey lay pressed against the stone floor of the balcony. He could feel it vibrating beneath him. He didn't know which sound was louder, the throbbing beat of the music or his heart pounding against his chest. He heard a rustle of movement and looked up to see Pablo crawling to the edge of the balcony.

Pablo peered over the edge of the balcony. He saw one guard leaning lazily against a car, and another guard fifty yards away and holding a phone to his ear.

Satisfied that no one was watching, Pablo squatted on his haunches, tied one end of the knotted sheets to a metal railing on the balcony and tossed the other end over the side.

"Marisol, you're first," he whispered. "When you reach the ground, lay down flat."

"So the guards don't see me?" she said.

"So you don't get hit by any stray bullets."

Marisol nodded. "Wish me luck."

She stood up quickly, slipped a lithe leg over the railing, then another and took hold of the sheets. Gripping the sheets tightly, she crossed her ankles, kept her legs angled towards the house and inched her way down, lowering one hand and then the other.

Pablo watched her from above, his head protruding over the edge of the balcony. He kept one eye on Marisol and another on the guards.

Marisol kept a steady pace, grunting from the exertion. Her feet touched down. She let go of the sheets, waved up at Pablo, and dropped flat on the ground.

Pablo turned to Jeffrey. "Marisol made it. Now it's your turn."

Jeffrey's voice was shaky. "Are you sure? What if the sheets break?"

"Then I guess I'll have to jump."

"I meant for me."

"You'll break a leg, maybe two, and then we're all dead."

Jeffrey frowned and stared down at the balcony floor.

"Jeffrey?" Pablo said and his friend looked up. "We'll miss the plane."

Jeffrey nodded. "How do I do this?"

"Keep your hands close to each other and your arms tight against your body." Pablo demonstrated. "Your lower body should be angled in, like a jackknife. You can even cross your ankles if it helps. Then just lower yourself down, one hand after the other. When you touch ground, lay down flat. Easy as pie."

Jeffrey started to rise. Pablo gripped his arm and looked him in the eye. "If you fall, no matter how bad it hurts, don't make a sound. Just keep still. I'll come and find you."

Jeffrey grunted.

"And if you do fall," Pablo added, "try not to land on top of Marisol."

Jeffrey grunted again. He started to rise. Pablo grabbed his arm. "Hold on."

Pablo's eyes scanned the area. One guard was still on the phone, waving his free arm wildly, as if in an argument. The other guard had slid off the car and was walking away from them. "Okay," Pablo said.

With a lumbering movement, Jeffrey rose to his feet, lifted one leg over the balcony railing, paused, and then lifted his other leg over. He stood there, panting, his heart beginning to pound.

"Go on," Pablo said.

"I can't."

"You have to."

Jeffrey glanced at the desert ground, twenty feet below, and his head swooned.

"Don't look down!"

Jeffrey nodded. He gripped the sheets, and pulled his arms in tight against his ribcage, imitating what Pablo had shown him.

"One hand after the other," Pablo said.

Jeffrey lifted one foot gingerly off the balcony, tested his grip, and then lifted his other foot off. Immediately, his lower body dropped and he slammed into the balcony railing. His legs bicycled furiously.

"Go on," Pablo said.

Jeffrey lowered his upper hand just below the other and grabbed the sheets.

"That's it," Pablo said.

Jeffrey inched his way down, grunting and sucking in huge gulps of air. He hadn't lowered himself more than three feet before he felt his hands slipping and his strength giving out.

"Keep going," he heard Pablo whisper from above.

Jeffrey could no longer keep his arms close to his body. His weight sagged and his arms stretched out. He felt the sheets slipping through his hands and he fell.

He hit the ground with a splat. For a second, he couldn't breathe, then a searing pain shot through his ankle and he wanted to scream.

Something soft rustled up against him. A warm female hand clamped over his mouth, pressing down on his lips. "Shhh," Marisol whispered in his ear.

Pablo peered over the balcony from above. Behind him, three loud knocks sounded at the bedroom door.

Jeffrey inhaled sharply, his ankle throbbing. Marisol lay almost on top of him. Her soft hair brushed against his face, her breath tickled his ear. "Shhh."

Marisol raised her head and glanced upward. A moment ago she had seen the outline of Pablo's head peeking out over the edge of the balcony, but now he was gone.

Pablo crouched in the shadows of the balcony, his eyes on the bedroom door. The knock sounded again, louder this time.

Pablo glanced at the bed sheets tied to the balcony railing. If someone came in the room, they'd see the open window and the sheets trailing to the ground. He swung the window frame closed. Chips of broken glass tinkled down. He reached for the sheets.

Gunshots boomed outside the bedroom door. Bullets ripped through the doorknob and lock.

Marisol lurched and started to scream. Jeffrey clasped his hand over her mouth and pulled her down on top of him. He held her thrashing body against his chest, his heart thudding wildly.

Pablo watched wide-eyed from the balcony as the bedroom door was kicked open and Thomas strode into the room, carrying an AK-47. He went straight to the control panel, and checked the video monitors. The images were cloudy with gas. He pressed the intercom button. "Still alive?" When no response came, he turned away from the vault with a smirk. Pablo leaned back in the shadows.

Jeffrey removed his hand from Marisol's mouth. She whispered frantically, "We have to help Pablo."

"There's not much we can do down here," Jeffrey said.

Marisol reached for the bed sheets. "I'm going back up."

"Wait. Give him a minute."

They both looked up at the balcony.

Pablo watched as Thomas sat on the side of the bed and pulled a phone from his pocket. He didn't seem to notice that the bed sheets were missing, and he hadn't glanced once at the broken window.

As Thomas played with his phone, Pablo sprang to his feet, swung his legs deftly over the railing, and grasped the bed sheets. In a second, he was gone, lowering himself, hand-by-hand, down the makeshift escape route.

Jeffrey and Marisol watched from the ground.

"He's coming," Jeffrey whispered.

When he was still three feet off the ground, Pablo let go of the sheets, dropped to his feet, and sprawled out on the ground, next to Jeffrey and Marisol.

Marisol gripped his arm. "Are you okay?"

Pablo nodded. "It was Thomas. He wanted to make sure we were dead."

"Jeffrey's hurt," Marisol said.

Pablo turned to his friend.

"My ankle," Jeffrey said. "I don't know if I can walk."

"You have to," Pablo said. "Susie's life depends on it." He raised his head and scanned the area for the guards. Neither was in sight.

"Which ankle is it?" Pablo asked.

"My left."

"Marisol, take his right arm."

Marisol scooted under Jeffrey's right arm. Pablo put Jeffrey's left arm over his shoulder. "On three," he said.

Pablo counted and they all rose to their feet. Jeffrey winced, holding his left foot off the ground. Music blared from the house. The moon and stars blazed down from above. The three friends hobbled their way to the idling plane.

Chapter Twenty-Eight

Wolfe leaned back against the cockpit door. "Cry all you want, it won't bring your friends back to life."

Susie sniffled and used her free hand to wipe her eyes. "You're going to hell."

Wolfe smiled broadly. "Your friends are already there."

"No, they're not!"

Wolfe's smile vanished. He stepped forward and glared down at the girl. "You have a smart mouth, don't you?" He reached down, grabbed hold of Susie's hair and twisted it sharply.

Susie cried out.

The little dogs yelped loudly.

The cockpit door opened and Clarisse stepped out.

"What are you doing?"

"I'm teaching your friend here some manners." Wolfe pulled Susie's hair, tilting her head back. She grimaced in pain. Wolfe leaned in close and whispered in her ear. "Just wait until we get this plane in the air. I'll come back here and pay you a visit. You'll be singing a different tune by the time we land, I promise you that."

"Leave her alone," Clarisse said.

Wolfe released Susie's hair. He stared down at her for moment, and then headed towards the front of the plane. As he stepped past Clarisse, he gave her a shove and passed behind her and into the cockpit.

The one-eyed man sat in the copilot's seat, checking the plane's instruments and preparing for takeoff. Wolfe stepped behind him and plopped down in the pilot's seat with a heavy sigh. The one-eyed man gave him a crooked grin. "I can manage the takeoff if you'd prefer to entertain your little friend."

Wolfe shook his head. "No offense, but I'm not putting my life in the hands of a one-eyed pilot."

The one-eyed man laughed uproariously.

Thirty yards from the plane, lying flat on their bellies on the desert ground, Jeffrey, Pablo and Marisol watched as a hatch opened at the rear of the aircraft. It was dark inside the plane and they saw no one.

"That must be Clarisse," said Pablo. "Come on."

He and Marisol hoisted Jeffrey to his feet, put his arms over their shoulders, and pressed forward. As they neared the plane, Clarisse stepped into view in the open hatch. Pablo and Marisol stopped below the hatch. Straining under the weight, they hoisted Jeffrey up and into Clarisse's arms. Pablo and Marisol grunted and pushed, Clarisse grunted and pulled, and finally Jeffrey was onboard.

Pablo laced his fingers together. Marisol put her hands on his shoulders and placed one foot on his hands. She straightened her leg, and Pablo boosted her up and into the plane.

Jeffrey and Marisol each lowered an arm out of the hatch. Pablo leapt and caught hold of them. His legs pedaled furiously as his friends pulled him up and into the plane. They scrambled to their feet, with Jeffrey favoring his injured ankle. He turned to Clarisse and whispered, "Where's Susie?"

Clarisse lifted a finger to her lips. With her other hand, she pointed to the front of the plane. Jeffrey nodded. Clarisse closed the hatch door behind them, and then shooed them with the back of her hand into a small kitchen. As they filed into the room, Clarisse disappeared up the aisle.

From the copilot's seat, the one-eyed man twisted his torso and called over his shoulder, "Clarisse!"

The girl appeared in the cockpit doorway.

"Find a seat and buckle in," the one-eyed man said.

Clarisse nodded and stepped out.

Wolfe readied the plane for takeoff. "We're on our way," he said.

Susie sat whimpering in her plane seat. Clarisse stepped down the aisle and took the seat directly behind her. She leaned forward and whispered in Susie's ear. "Your friends are onboard."

Susie turned to her, wide-eyed. "They're alive?"

"Shhh." Clarisse nodded towards the cockpit. "We're taking off." She pulled her seat belt across her body and buckled in.

Pablo flipped a light switch in the kitchen. A dim light filled the room.

"Pablo, I'm scared," Marisol whispered.

"I thought danger was your middle name?"

"Not now."

He put his arm around her and pulled her body against his.

Jeffrey surveyed the room: counters, cabinets, a sink, and a small refrigerator.

The plane began to move.

"We're taking off," Pablo said.

The three of them slid down and seated themselves on the floor, bracing their backs against the cabinets.

Outside, the plane moved down the desert runway.

In the tiny kitchen, Jeffrey studied his friends. Marisol's eyes were closed, her body curled into a ball and leaning against Pablo, his arm around her shoulders. Pablo's face was stoic and staring straight ahead, but Jeffrey knew he was scared. How could he not be?

The plane picked up speed. Jeffrey felt his spine and the back of his head pressing hard into the cabinet behind him.

With its outside lights flashing, the plane hurtled down the runway, faster and faster, and then lifted up into the night air.

Jeffrey felt a leap in his stomach, like the rest of his body had just lifted off the ground, but his stomach had remained behind. He glanced at his friends.

Both Pablo and Marisol had their eyes closed now. Jeffrey joined them, wishing he were anywhere else. But he wasn't, and now there was no turning back. The plane was inflight and they were onboard.

"What's our plan now?"

The voice was Pablo's.

Jeffrey opened his eyes. Pablo and Marisol sat across from him on the floor of the plane's kitchen, their eyes pleading for an answer. The drone of the plane's engine was the only sound.

Jeffrey straightened his glasses. "We'll have to convince them to land the plane and let us all go, including Susie."

"How are we going to do that?"

"I have no idea."

Pablo sprang to his feet and rummaged through the kitchen drawers. He found paper plates, napkins and packets of instant soup, and tossed them all aside. He spoke to his friends: "See if you can find a knife or a fork, or something to fight with."

Jeffrey grabbed hold of the kitchen counter and pulled himself to his feet. The counter groaned and creaked under his weight. He opened a cabinet above the sink, but found only plastic straws and more packets of instant soup.

Marisol turned to the small refrigerator next to her and opened its door. "Nothing in here, but soda and water."

"Cans or bottles?" asked Pablo.

"One can of soda and some plastic bottles of water."

"Give me the soda."

Marisol took the soda can from the refrigerator and handed it to him. Pablo sat on the floor, removed his shoe, and slipped off his sock.

"What are you doing?" Marisol said.

"You'll see."

Pablo slipped the can inside his sock and hoisted it. The can slid down to the bottom of the sock. "Remember what Eddie Lee told us, Jeffrey?" He held the top of the sock with his right hand and slapped the improvised blackjack against his left palm with a thwack. "Now I've got a weapon."

Jeffrey's eyes widened. "Marisol, give me one of those waters."

She handed him a plastic water bottle.

Jeffrey slid down to the floor. Imitating Pablo, he removed his shoe and sock, and slid the plastic water bottle inside his sock. He held the sock by the top and slapped it against his palm. "Now I've got a weapon too."

"I'm not wearing any socks," Marisol said.

"Use your fingernails," Pablo said. "Go for the eyes and throat. It's going to be us or them."

Outside, the plane climbed higher and higher in the night sky.

Susie twisted her body as best as she could in her passenger seat and whispered to Clarisse behind her. "What's going on?"

Clarisse did not answer. She turned in her own seat and looked to the rear of the plane.

In the cockpit, a cell phone rang. Wolfe glanced suspiciously at his copilot as the one-eyed man fished a phone from his pocket and answered it: "Yes?" His eye squinted as he pressed the phone harder against his ear. "Speak louder. I can't hear you."

Thomas stood on the balcony of the desert house, holding a phone to his ear. His other hand fumbled with the trail of bed sheets tied to the balcony railing. Music blared from the house beneath him. He shouted into the phone. "The fat kid and his friends; I think they got away."

The one-eyed man sat up sharply. "Impossible!"

Wolfe shot the one-eyed man a quizzical look.

The one-eyed man spoke into the phone. "They're locked in the vault."

Thomas flicked the bed sheets over the balcony rail and stared out over the expanse of desert before him. "Somebody tied a couple of sheets together and climbed out the window."

The one-eyed man raised an eyebrow. "Your friends perhaps?"

"Not my friends."

"What is it?" Wolfe asked.

The one-eyed man waved at Wolfe to keep quiet, and spoke sharply into the phone. "Check the cameras."

"I did. I couldn't see anything. The vault is filled with gas."

"Then they are dead."

"I'm telling you, somebody tied bed sheets together and climbed out the window. I think they got away."

The one-eyed man gripped the phone tightly. "Search the grounds. If you find them, kill them immediately." He hung up.

Wolfe turned to him. "What was that all about?"

"Just a minor inconvenience."

Thomas returned his phone to his pocket. Shouts from the ground drew his attention. He saw patrol guards running to the front of the house.

Moving swiftly, Thomas stepped back into the bedroom, crossed to the open door and went across the hall to a bedroom facing the front of the house. The shouts from outside were louder now.

Thomas opened the window and stepped out on the balcony. He surveyed the front yard and the road in front of the house. His eyes widened with growing disbelief as he saw, far off down the road, the lights of a slowly approaching police cruiser, followed by another cruiser, and another. It was a never-ending procession of police cars, red and blue lights spinning and popping silently atop their hoods. All of them moving steadily forward, headed straight for the house.

The patrol guards in front of the house took cover behind vehicles, aimed their automatic weapons, and opened fire at the line of police cars.

The procession of police cruisers stopped, and then fanned out to the sides. Moments later came return fire.

Bullets pinged off cars and struck the house. A bullet hit the window behind Thomas and shattered it. Thomas raised his AK-47 to his shoulder and pulled the trigger.

In the cockpit of the plane, the one-eyed man turned his head to the side and shouted over his shoulder. "Clarisse!"

In a moment, the girl was at the cockpit door. Both men eyed her carefully.

"Tell me something," the one-eyed man said, "why did you go back to the house before we took off?"

"I told you, I had to use the bathroom."

"And I told you we have a bathroom on the plane."

"I don't like using it."

Both men watched her, their faces tightening.

Clarisse sensed their suspicion and laughed nervously. "I had to go."

"Tell me something else," the one-eyed man said, "did you let your friends out of the vault?"

"Me? No! How could I do that? I don't know the combination."

"That's right, you don't. But your fat friend is very clever, isn't he?"

Clarisse laughed. "He's not *that* clever."

"Oh, yes, he is. And you don't seem overly concerned about his death, do you?"

Clarisse shrugged. "If he's dead, he's dead."

"Yes. *If* he is dead." He reached inside his jacket to a holster on his hip and removed a gun.

Clarisse saw the weapon and her eyes widened.

"You might be telling the truth," the one-eyed man said, "and you might be lying. All the same, I think I'll have a quick look around the plane."

"There's nothing to look for," Clarisse said.

"I'll be the judge of that." The one-eyed man rose out of his seat.

"I'll go with you," Clarisse said.

"You'll stay here," Wolfe said. He grabbed her by the arm and pulled her roughly into the co-pilot's seat.

"This is crazy," Clarisse said.

"We'll know very soon," the one-eyed man said.

"You don't trust me now?" said Clarisse, her voice rising. "Are you going to handcuff me too, like the other girl?"

"If you don't shut up, I will," Wolfe said. He nodded with his chin at the gun in the one-eyed man's hand. "Be careful with that thing. You could shoot out a window and decompress the entire plane."

The one-eyed man nodded and returned the gun to his holster. He reached into the inside breast pocket of his jacket and pulled out his switchblade knife.

"Can't you see how crazy this is?" Clarisse said.

The one-eyed man eyed her coldly. "I believe the lady doth protest too much." He pressed the button on the knife handle and the blade jumped out and locked into place.

Clarisse eyed the glistening blade. The one-eyed man noticed her look and stepped out of the cockpit.

The one-eyed man stepped into the cabin and approached the passenger seats. When the dogs saw him, they yelped enthusiastically. The man stopped in front of Susie and eyed her suspiciously.

"What?" she said, noticing the knife in his hand.

He stepped past her and she glanced fearfully over her shoulder.

The man proceeded slowly down the aisle, glancing down each row of seats, left and right. Susie called after him, "What are you doing?"

The one-eyed man ignored her and bent down to peer under a row of seats.

"Are you looking for ghosts?" Susie said loudly, hoping her voice would carry to the back of the plane.

Clarisse heard Susie's voice and turned in her seat towards the cockpit door. "You're looking for ghosts?" she said loudly.

Wolfe backhanded her across the mouth. Clarisse shrieked.

From the kitchen, Jeffrey and his friends heard Susie's voice and Clarisse's muffled scream.

"Someone's coming," Pablo whispered. He, Jeffrey and Marisol stood stiff as boards, listening, waiting.

In the cockpit, Clarisse sat sobbing, her lip bloodied. Wolfe glanced over his shoulder and out the cockpit door.

The one-eyed man reached the last row of seats. He glanced down the row to his left and to his right. All he saw were black satchels, loaded down with money. He bent down and poked his head under the seats. Nothing.

In the kitchen, Jeffrey leaned back against the counter. It creaked loudly. Pablo and Marisol turned to him with alarm in their eyes.

The one-eyed man heard the creak and straightened up. He listened. The monotonous drone of the plane's engine was the only sound now. His nostrils flared.

Susie sat twisted around in her plane seat, watching his every move.

Ahead of the one-eyed man, a dim light shone from the kitchen. His eyes narrowed. He tightened his grip on the knife and stepped towards the kitchen light.

Jeffrey and his friends tensed.

The one-eyed man stepped slowly to the kitchen entrance and turned into the open doorway. Jeffrey, Pablo, and Marisol stood directly in front of him, huddled together and staring at him with wide-open eyes. For one startled second, the man froze, and then his yellow-tinged eye settled on Jeffrey. *"You?"*

"You," Jeffrey said.

Pablo stepped forward and swung. His homemade blackjack hit the one-eyed man on the bridge of his nose. A stream of blood spurted from the man's nostrils. Pablo swung again, hitting the man across the temple. Jeffrey joined in, their improvised weapons whistling through the air and landing with dull thuds.

The man covered his head with one arm and slashed his knife wildly with the other. He staggered backed into the aisle of the plane. Pablo and Jeffrey followed right behind him, pummeling the man over the head and shoulders with their weapons.

Susie saw them and screamed.

In the cockpit, Wolfe and Clarisse turned to each other. Wolfe's face flushed red with anger.

A blow from Pablo struck the one-eyed man across the forehead and he stumbled backwards and fell. Jeffrey and Pablo stood over him, raining down their blackjacks on his head and face.

Wolfe reached inside his jacket to his shoulder holster and pulled his service revolver.

Clarisse grabbed for it and Wolfe shoved her back. He bolted from his seat and out the cockpit door. Clarisse followed him.

Wolfe saw the one-eyed man sprawled on the floor at the rear of the plane, Jeffrey and Pablo standing over him, pelting him with their weapons, and Marisol behind them. He pointed his gun at the boys.

Susie screamed, "No!"

Clarisse leapt on Wolfe's back and clawed at his eyes.

Pablo leaped over the one-eyed man's body and sprinted up the aisle.

Wolfe grabbed at Clarisse's fingers. His body twisted back. Susie grabbed hold of his hair with her free hand and pulled him further backwards.

Pablo dropped his blackjack and lunged for the man's gun. He grabbed Wolfe by the wrist. The detective's arm twisted inward and a shot fired. Wolfe's body jerked and then sagged. He crumpled to the floor. Blood seeped out of a hole in his chest and onto the carpeted floor of the plane.

Pablo kneeled quickly beside Wolfe's body. He felt for a pulse and laid his ear on the massive chest, listening for a heartbeat. Finding none, he stood and stared down at the lifeless body. "This one's dead," he announced.

Jeffrey dropped his homemade blackjack and kneeled by the side of the one-eyed man. He felt for a pulse on the man's wrist and the side of his neck. The man lay motionless, his face bloodied to a pulp, his yellow-tinged eye staring dull and lifeless.

Jeffrey stood up. Marisol stood next to him, her hand on his shoulder, staring in horror at the man's body. Jeffrey looked toward the front of the plane and called to Pablo, "So is this one."

Susie twisted around in her seat. "Somebody uncuff me!"

Clarisse fished a set of keys from Wolfe's pants pocket and hurried to Susie.

Pablo sprang towards the cockpit and stopped in the doorway. Ahead of him, both pilot seats were empty. Through the windshield, the night sky was black as coal, save for the beam of the plane's headlights. The only sound was the purr of the plane's engine. Pablo stared at the plane's controls and called out behind him, "Clarisse, do you know how to fly this thing?"

Clarisse unlocked Susie's handcuffs and faced the cockpit. "What? No!"

Jeffrey limped quickly up the aisle, followed by Marisol.

Pablo turned from the cockpit door and faced his friends.

"This plane's going down," he said. "And we're going down with it."

Chapter Twenty-Nine

The color drained from Jeffrey's face. He turned to Clarisse. "Where are the parachutes?"

"Parachutes?" Susie said, her voice rising. "You mean, we have to jump?"

"We jump or we die," Pablo said.

Clarisse stepped quickly to a cabinet by the side of the cockpit door. She yanked open the cabinet door and four parachute packs tumbled to the floor.

Marisol stared down at the packs with horror-stricken eyes. "I only see four parachutes."

"And there are five of us," Susie said.

"That's all we brought," Clarisse explained, "two parachutes for the pilots, one for me, and one for Susie."

All eyes turned to Jeffrey.

Pablo's jaw tightened. "Think fast, Jeffrey."

"The solution is simple," Jeffrey said, his voice shaking. "Two people are going to have to jump together."

"What? That's impossible!" Susie said.

"Either that," Jeffrey said, pausing to look at the frightened faces around him, "either that or somebody has to stay behind."

Marisol and Susie gasped.

The plane bucked. The girls screamed and everyone lurched to the side.

When they regained their balance, Jeffrey grabbed three parachute packs and handed one each to Pablo, Susie and Clarisse.

A lone parachute pack lay on the floor of the plane. Marisol watched with ever widening eyes as Jeffrey picked up the last pack, stepped towards her, and held it out for her to take.

"No, Jeffrey," she said.

"Take it," he insisted.

"No, I won't!"

Susie and Clarisse watched, hesitating.

Jeffrey saw them and yelled, "Put those parachutes on!"

"How?" Susie said, fumbling with her pack.

"Put the pack on your back and your arms and your legs through the straps," Pablo said, demonstrating. "When you jump, pull the handle." He pointed to the ripcord on his parachute. "And when you hit the ground, roll over so you don't break your leg."

"Have you done this before, Pablo?" Susie asked.

"No, but I've seen it in a movie."

"Hurry up," Jeffrey said. He turned to Marisol and thrust the parachute pack at her.

Marisol backed away, her body trembling. "You take it, Jeffrey."

"It's yours," he said.

"No, it's yours."

"This whole thing is my fault," Jeffrey said. "None of us would be here if it wasn't for me. Take it."

Marisol stamped her foot. "No, Jeffrey! I won't do it!"

"Take it!" Jeffrey shoved the parachute into her arms.

"No!" Marisol threw the pack on the floor and burst into tears.

Pablo grabbed Marisol by the arm and pulled her body up against his, the two of them face to face. "Jeffrey, tie us together," he said, "and put that parachute on."

Jeffrey pulled off his belt and looped it around both Pablo and Marisol.

"What if that belt breaks?" Susie said.

Jeffrey turned to her. "Put your parachute on."

"It is on."

Jeffrey pulled the belt taut, pressing Pablo and Marisol's bodies tightly together, and buckled it. Marisol looked up into Pablo's eyes, inches away from her own.

"Pablo, if I die, it will be with you."

"We're not gonna die," Pablo said. "At least, I hope not. Jeffrey, hurry up with that parachute."

Jeffrey grabbed the last parachute and strapped it on.

"What if we land in the ocean?" Susie said.

"Swim," Pablo answered.

"I don't know how."

Jeffrey and Pablo exchanged a look, but said nothing.

Jeffrey surveyed them all. "Okay," he said, and led the way to the hatch at the back of the plane. The others followed behind him, Pablo and Marisol shuffling their way together.

"How do we know we're not going to get sucked out of here when that door opens?" Pablo said. "I've seen that in a movie too."

"It depends on how fast we're going," Jeffrey said. "We haven't been in the air long. Hold on to your ripcords. If we fly out the door, pull it."

Everyone's hands went immediately to their ripcords.

"Wait," Susie cried, "what about the dogs?"

"Who cares about the dogs?"

"We can't just leave them here to die."

Jeffrey sighed. He ran down the aisle to the front of the plane's passenger seats, grabbed the three traveling cases containing Yankee, Doodle and Dandy, and ran back. He handed a case to Clarisse and two cases to Susie. Susie gripped the handles on the cases with one hand and kept her other hand on her ripcord.

"Now let's go," Jeffrey said. He turned to Clarisse. "How do we open this door?"

Clarisse stepped forward and unlocked the hatch. She and Jeffrey took hold of it. Jeffrey turned to his friends.

"Ready?"

Heads nodded.

"On three," Jeffrey said. "One, two ..."

The others watched, tense and waiting.

"... three."

Jeffrey and Clarisse opened the hatch door. A roaring wind blasted through the open hatch and shook the plane. Susie screamed. The dogs yelped and rattled their travel cases. The wind ripped through the cabin and tore open the satchels on the passenger seats. Currency flew out of the satchels, around the cabin and out the open door.

Jeffrey and his friends teetered, trying to find their balance. They looked at each other, frightened and unable to move. A blizzard of currency swirled over their heads. Outside the open door, was a world of black nothingness.

"Who's going first?" Jeffrey shouted above the roar.

Four frightened faces stared back at him. The plane lurched, causing them all to sway. The girls screamed.

"Somebody has to go first!" Jeffrey shouted.

"We'll go," Pablo said. Marisol looked up at his eyes and he gave her a short nod. They shuffled their way to the open hatch.

"We'll see you on the ground," Jeffrey yelled, and gave them a thumbs-up.

Pablo gave him a thumbs-up back. He put one hand on his rip-cord and placed his other arm around Marisol, squeezing her body against his.

Marisol wrapped her arms around him. "Hold on to me, Pablo."

"I will."

"God, if I die," Pablo said, "please take me to Heaven." He made the sign of the cross and put his hand back on the ripcord.

"Me too," said Marisol, making the sign of the cross.

"Me three," said Susie.

"Let's go!" Pablo shouted, and he leapt out the open door with Marisol. Her scream lasted for a second and then it was gone.

"Oh my God," Jeffrey said, staring out the open hatch. At this moment, his friends were hurtling towards Earth. He blinked and turned to Susie. She stood with her back pressed up against the cabin wall. "You're next," Jeffrey said.

"No, you're next."

"No, *you're* next." He grabbed her by the arm and pulled her to the open hatch. The wind whipped their hair wildly and the roar swallowed their voices.

"I can't do it!"

"This plane's going down!"

"I don't care!"

"Go! Before we all die!"

"I can't!"

"You have to!"

"Ohhh!"

"Jump!"

"I can't!"

"Jump!"

"Ohhh! I hate you, Jeffrey Jones!""

"Jump!"

Susie screamed and leapt out the open hatch. In an instant, she was gone.

Jeffrey turned to Clarisse. Her face grew long with anguish and tears welled in her eyes. "What's going to happen to me if I die?"

"You're in a state of mortal sin. If you die, you're going straight to hell."

"I don't want to go to hell!" She burst out crying, howling and wailing like an animal in agony.

Jeffrey grabbed her by both arms and shook her. "Do you accept Jesus Christ," he shouted, "and the true Catholic faith? Do you?"

"Yes!"

Jeffrey limped quickly to the body of the one-eyed man. He found the improvised blackjack he'd dropped on the floor and pulled the water bottle out of his sock. He hurried back to Clarisse.

Jeffrey twisted the plastic cap off the water bottle and tilted Clarisse's head back. He poured water over her forehead as he spoke: "I baptize you in the name of the Father, and of the Son, and of the Holy Ghost."

The plane lurched violently. Clarisse screamed and fell out the open hatch into the night sky. Jeffrey grasped at the air as he tilted backwards. His feet came off the floor. He landed on his back and slid down the aisle. He felt a sharp crack on the crown of his skull as his head slammed into the back of passenger seat. Then everything went black.

Chapter Thirty

Jeffrey opened his eyes.

How long was he out? A second? A minute? An hour?

He was alone on the plane now. The others had all jumped and he was alone.

He felt an urge to close his eyes and drift off to sleep. It would be so easy. Just close his eyelids gently and drift off to sleep, never to awaken.

The plane shook and began to tilt, the rear end lifting higher and higher. The steady drone of the engine gave way to a high-pitched shriek. The plane was diving and taking him with it.

Panic seized him and his eyes opened wide. He had to get to the open hatch and jump before the plane crashed.

He tried to stand, but the floor underneath him tilted and fell back and tilted again. He tumbled further into the plane, rolling across the floor until his back slammed up against the far wall. A fuse box above his head exploded in a shower of fiery red sparks.

He screamed and covered his face and eyes. The shriek of the plane's engine was ear-shattering.

He forced his body to move, crawling slowly up the aisle. The floor tilted up at an impossible angle. He stretched and reached, stretched and reached, first his hand, then his knee. The plane was in free fall. In seconds, it would all be over.

He reached the hatch, panting and gasping for air. It was now or never. He made the sign of the cross and repeated Pablo's prayer: "God, if I die, please take me to Heaven." He took a deep breath and tumbled out the open door.

The smell of the plane's exhaust and the scream of its engine lasted for a second and then disappeared. Frigid wind whipped over his face and rustled his hair. He reached for the ripcord and pulled.

There was a rustle of nylon and a sharp tug under his armpits. His parachute billowed out above with a whoosh, pulling his body vertical. Ice cold wind snaked up the inside of his pant legs and up the inside of his shirt, chilling his body. He felt no sensation of falling, yet he knew that he was.

His eyes adjusted quickly to the darkness. The stars in the night sky never looked so bright. Cold, clean air filled his nostrils and lungs. Never in his life had he felt more truly alone and yet so alive. Was this what it was like to be a bird?

Seconds passed. He was struck by the utter silence. His mind flashed to his friends. By now they were all either safe on the ground ... or dead. Very soon he would be joining them, in life or in death.

Through the darkness, he saw the ground rising up fast to meet him. He saw no houses or trees, only open ground. He brought his feet together quickly and closed his eyes. *Please, God! Please! Let me live!*

It was the last thing he remembered.

Chapter 31 – Christmas Eve

His father's face was fuzzy, hovering overhead.

"Where am I?" Jeffrey muttered.

"You're back in L.A., buddy. You were airlifted here by helicopter."

Jeffrey blinked. Without his glasses, the hospital room was just a blur.

"Where are my glasses?"

His father reached for his glasses on the nightstand table and handed them to Jeffrey. Jeffrey slipped them over his nose and his father's face filled in clear and distinct. He glanced around the room. Outside the window, the sky was darkening. The smell of ammonia and disinfectant came to his nose and he grimaced.

"What day is it?"

"Christmas Eve, five o'clock. You've been out cold for the last sixteen hours."

Jeffrey shifted his body slightly on the bed and groaned. "I feel like I was hit by a truck."

"Just relax. Your mother was here. She's been worried frantic. She waited by your bedside for hours before she passed out. I called a cab and sent her home."

"Did you hear what happened?"

"Yup. Pablo told me all about it."

"He's alive?"

"He's in the waiting room with Marisol Rodriguez. They've been here with their families since noon, waiting for you to regain consciousness. I'll send them in." He rose out of his chair.

"Wait, what happened to the gangs and the counterfeit money?"

"It's been all over the news since late last night. There was a tremendous shootout. Miraculously, no cops were killed or hit by gunfire. They arrested over two hundred people and recovered hundreds of millions of dollars in counterfeit money. A couple of guys got away. The police, the Secret Service, the news agencies, they all want to talk to you."

Jeffrey groaned.

"It's okay," his father said, "that can wait till the morning." He stepped to the door.

"Dad?"

His father stopped and turned.

"Are you mad?"

His father smiled. "I'm not mad. I'm just thankful you're alive." He stepped out of the room.

Jeffrey lay back in the bed and breathed a sigh of relief. Minutes later, he heard his name called from the door. He looked up and saw Pablo and Marisol, locked arm-in-arm, with huge grins on their faces.

They entered and walked slowly to his bedside, Pablo walking with a noticeable limp and leaning on Marisol for support. Jeffrey spotted a huge cast on his ankle.

Tears welled in Marisol's eyes. She bent down to hug Jeffrey and her hair spilled over his face. The scent of her hair was fresh and overpowering. Jeffrey inhaled deeply and hugged her back.

Marisol straightened up. She smiled joyfully and wiped her eyes. Pablo extended his fist and Jeffrey bumped it with his own fist.

"We landed in a field," Pablo said, "and then hiked to some guy's house. Actually, Marisol hiked. I just held on."

"He couldn't walk," Marisol said, "so I had to do something."

"My ankle," Pablo explained. "The doctor says my football-playing days might be over."

"Oh no," said Jeffrey.

Pablo shrugged. "It was fun while it lasted."

"Susie?"

Pablo and Marisol exchanged knowing smiles.

"What?" Jeffrey said.

"Susie's okay," Pablo said. "She's a little shook up, but she's okay. She landed on a farm, in a pig sty."

Marisol swatted his arm playfully.

"She did!" Pablo said.

"Oh no," said Jeffrey.

"Oh yes," said Marisol. "She was covered in mud and rolling around with the pigs."

"Oh no," Jeffrey said again, smiling.

Marisol wagged her finger as she spoke. "She said, 'You tell that Jeffrey Jones I'll never speak to him again!' "

The three friends roared with laughter.

When the laugher died down, Jeffrey looked at them both.

"Clarisse?"

Pablo and Marisol exchanged another look. Marisol looked down, unable to meet Jeffrey's gaze.

Pablo looked Jeffrey straight in the eye.

"No," was all he said.

The clock at his bedside read 7:10 when Jeffrey awoke from a fitful sleep. It was early evening. He lay with his eyes closed, in the murky world between sleep and consciousness. Clarisse was on his mind: a sad and lonely girl who lived a sad and lonely life. He wondered if she made it to Heaven and his heart ached.

His mind drifted back to the first time he saw her at the hospital. He remembered how he and Pablo followed her to the stairwell. How they encountered Kevin Wong's killer in the same hospital stairwell ... the intense stare of the killer's eyes. A thought flashed across Jeffrey's mind and suddenly he was wide awake. He grabbed his glasses off the nightstand table and put them on.

The room was dark, but he made out Pablo and Marisol, asleep in a pair of chairs to his side, Pablo's head on Marisol's shoulder.

"Pablo!" Jeffrey whispered with urgency in his voice. "Pablo, wake up!"

Pablo stirred and rubbed his eyes. "What is it?"

"Have you seen my dad?"

"He went home to check on your mom. He said he'd be back." Pablo checked his watch. "We better get home too."

"Wait, remember the killer at the hospital? Who does he remind you of?"

Pablo furrowed his brow.

"Think," Jeffrey said. "It's important. What do you remember?"

234 / Mike Mains

"Well, he had those eyes ..."

"You called them rattlesnake eyes."

"Right. That's what they reminded me of."

"Who else has those eyes?"

"Nobody I know."

"There is somebody you know. Remember, the killer was wearing a surgical mask and pretending to be a doctor. We couldn't see his face below his eyes."

"Right."

"Who else would look like the killer if you covered the lower half of his face?"

Pablo thought for a few seconds and then suddenly sat straight up. "Thomas?"

"Exactly. His face is so ugly, with those pockmarks and that crooked nose, that you never notice his eyes. But if he covered up the lower half of his face ..."

"... he would look just like the killer we saw. He has those same rattlesnake eyes. But he's in jail, isn't he?"

"Maybe, maybe not. My dad told me that a couple of guys got away. If Thomas was one of them, what would he be thinking right now?"

"He'd be thinking revenge. He'd be thinking of sneaking in here, just like he snuck into that other hospital. And he wouldn't waste any time either."

The two boys stared at each other for a moment then Pablo rose to his feet and shook Marisol by the shoulder.

"What happened?" she grumbled.

"Wake up," Pablo said quietly. "We have to move Jeffrey." He turned to his friend. "Can you walk?"

"No, but if you can get me to the elevator, I can make it to the lobby and take a cab home."

Pablo turned to Marisol. "We think Thomas is the one who killed Kevin Wong at the county hospital. And if he got away last night, we think he might be coming here to kill Jeffrey."

Marisol gasped.

"We'll have to move his bed," Pablo said.

Marisol rose quickly and went to the side of Jeffrey's bed. Pablo went to the other side.

"There should be wheels down there," Jeffrey said. "If you can unlock those, you can roll me down the hall and I'll hop off into the elevator."

Marisol gripped the hard metal latch and tried to release it. "This metal is cutting into my hands."

"I'll get a towel," Pablo said. He ducked into the bathroom.

Marisol glanced towards the door and gasped. A solitary figure stood in the doorway. Jeffrey looked and recognized the figure at once. It was Thomas Chan, dressed in the same white doctor's coat and surgical mask as before, and holding a gun in his hand. He stepped silently into the room.

Pablo emerged from the bathroom, saw Thomas, and stepped back, hiding in the shadows.

Marisol remained by the side of the bed, watching Thomas with terror-stricken eyes.

Jeffrey sat up in bed, his back pressed against the pillows and the wall behind him, pushing back with all his might.

Thomas leveled his gun. Above the surgical mask, his eyebrows slanted down sharply and his eyes burned intensely. "You thought you got away, didn't you, fat boy?"

236 / Mike Mains

"Just go," Jeffrey said. "Just run away. I won't tell anyone you've been here."

"I'm not going anywhere. Not until you're dead."

"Haven't enough people died already?"

"Yes, and one more is about to join them." Thomas raised his weapon and took aim.

Pablo sprang on one leg from the darkness and grabbed the wrist of Thomas's gun hand. Thomas's arm raised and a bullet fired, striking the wall just above Jeffrey's head.

Marisol screamed.

Pablo kept one hand on Thomas's wrist and swung his other arm around the young man's neck. The two of them tumbled to the floor. Jeffrey rolled off the bed on top of both of them.

Pablo pressed Thomas's gun hand to the floor. Another shot fired.

Jeffrey gripped Thomas's forehead from behind and pulled, straining the young man's neck.

Marisol ran around the back of the bed. She saw the gun in Thomas's hand and stepped on his fingers with all her weight. Thomas cried out and released the gun. Marisol snatched it up and stepped back.

Pablo let go of Thomas's wrist and fired punches with lightning speed at his face and head. In seconds, it was over. The would-be assassin lay unconscious on the floor.

Marisol grabbed the phone on the nightstand and called the police.

Jeffrey and Pablo kneeled on the floor, panting and heaving for air.

"Good thing he didn't see me," Pablo said.

"Yes," Jeffrey mused, "there's always the unexpected."

The two boys looked at each other and Pablo gave Jeffrey a pat on the back.

From somewhere down the hall floated the faint melody of *O Little Town of Bethlehem.*

O little town of Bethlehem
How still we see thee lie
Above thy deep and dreamless sleep
The silent stars go by

THANK YOU VERY MUCH for buying this book. If you enjoyed it, please share your thoughts by posting a review on Amazon or wherever you purchased the book. People often make their book-reading decisions based on other people's reviews (I know I do), and your review of this book could be the deciding factor for someone who is wondering whether or not to read it. Even a short, one sentence review will help. Thank you again.

The North Hollywood Detective Club Series

THE CASE OF THE HOLLYWOOD ART HEIST

Jeffrey Jones is a kid with a problem. A *lot* of problems. He's laughed at in school. The neighborhood bully has it out for him. And his parents treat him like a six-year-old. However, Jeffrey does have one ace up his sleeve: He's a master investigator.

When the brother of a classmate is arrested for stealing a valuable painting, Jeffrey and his best friend, Pablo Reyes, form The North Hollywood Detective Club and set out to rescue him from jail. Their investigation leads them to a mysterious tattoo parlor, a glamorous television star, and a 20-year-old unsolved murder!

THE CASE OF THE DEAD MAN'S TREASURE

A treasure worth killing for. Hired by their teacher to find the driver responsible for a hit-and-run car accident, teen detectives Jeffrey Jones and Pablo Reyes stumble upon a search for an ancient treasure worth two hundred million dollars. Working feverishly to decipher the clues to the treasure's location, they find themselves in a race against time with a ruthless treasure hunter who will stop at nothing to get his hands on the prize.

Mike Mains writes mystery and adventure books for sleuths of all ages. He can be reached at mainsmike@yahoo.com

Or via snail mail at: Mike Mains, 616 South Catalina Street, Suite 8, Los Angeles, California 90005.

Made in the USA
Monee, IL
16 December 2019